ROUND THE RED LAMP

ARTHUR CONAN DOYLE

ROUND THE RED LAMP.

BEHIND THE TIMES.

My first interview with Dr. James Winter was under dramatic circumstances. It occurred at two in the morning in the bedroom of an old country house. I kicked him twice on the white waistcoat and knocked off his gold spectacles, while he with the aid of a female accomplice stifled my angry cries in a flannel petticoat and thrust me into a warm bath. I am told that one of my parents, who happened to be present, remarked in a whisper that there was nothing the matter with my lungs. I cannot recall how Dr. Winter looked at the time, for I had other things to think of, but his description of my own appearance is far from flattering. A fluffy head, a body like a trussed goose, very bandy legs, and feet with the soles turned inwards—those are the main items which he can remember.

From this time onwards the epochs of my life were the periodical assaults which Dr. Winter made upon me. He vaccinated me; he cut me for an abscess; he blistered me for mumps. It was a world of peace and he the one dark cloud that threatened. But at last there came a time of real illness—a time when I lay for months together inside my wickerwork-basket bed, and then it was that I learned that that hard face could relax, that those country-made creaking boots could steal very gently to a bedside, and that that rough voice could thin into a whisper when it spoke to a sick child.

And now the child is himself a medical man, and yet Dr. Winter is the same as ever. I can see no change since first I can remember him, save that perhaps the brindled hair is a trifle whiter, and the huge shoulders a little more bowed. He is a very tall man, though he loses a couple of inches from his stoop. That big back of his has curved itself over sick beds until it has set in that shape. His face is of a walnut brown, and tells of long winter drives over bleak country roads, with the wind and the rain in his teeth. It looks smooth at a little distance, but as you approach him you see that it is shot with innumerable fine wrinkles like a last year's apple. They are hardly to be seen when he is in repose; but when he laughs his face breaks like a starred glass, and you realise then that though he looks old, he must be older than he looks.

How old that is I could never discover. I have often tried to find out, and have struck his stream as high up as George IV and even the Regency, but without ever getting quite to the source. His mind must have been open to impressions very early, but it must also have closed early, for the politics of the day have little interest for him, while he is fiercely excited about questions which are entirely prehistoric. He shakes his head when he speaks of the first Reform Bill and expresses grave doubts as to its wisdom, and I have heard him, when he was warmed by a glass of wine, say bitter things about Robert Peel and his abandoning of the Corn Laws. The death of that statesman brought the history of England to a definite close, and Dr. Winter refers to everything which had happened since then as to an insignificant anticlimax.

But it was only when I had myself become a medical man that I was able to appreciate how entirely he is a survival of a past generation. He had learned his medicine under that obsolete and forgotten system by which a youth was apprenticed to a surgeon, in the days when the study of anatomy was often approached through a violated grave. His views upon his own profession are even more reactionary than in politics. Fifty years have brought him little and deprived him of less. Vaccination was well within the teaching of his youth, though I think he has a secret preference for inoculation. Bleeding he would practise freely but for public opinion. Chloroform he regards as a dangerous innovation, and he always clicks with his tongue when it is mentioned. He has even been known to say vain things about Laennec, and to refer to the stethoscope as "a new-fangled French toy." He carries one in his hat out of deference to the expectations of his patients, but he is very hard of hearing, so that it makes little difference whether he uses it or not.

He reads, as a duty, his weekly medical paper, so that he has a general idea as to the advance of modern science. He always persists in looking upon it as a huge and rather ludicrous experiment. The germ theory of disease set him chuckling for a long time, and his favourite joke in the sick room was to say, "Shut the door or the germs will be getting in." As to the Darwinian theory, it struck him as being the crowning joke of the century. "The children in the nursery and the ancestors in the stable," he would cry, and laugh the tears out of his eyes.

He is so very much behind the day that occasionally, as things move round in their usual circle, he finds himself, to his bewilderment, in the front of the fashion. Dietetic treatment, for example, had been much in vogue in his youth, and he has more practical knowledge of it than any one whom I have met. Massage, too, was familiar to him when it was new to our generation. He had been trained also at a time when instruments were in a rudimentary state, and when men learned to trust more to their own fingers. He has a model surgical hand, muscular in the palm, tapering in the fingers, "with an eye at the end of each." I shall not easily forget how Dr. Patterson and I cut Sir John Sirwell, the County Member, and were unable to find the stone. It was a horrible moment. Both our careers were at stake. And then it was that Dr. Winter, whom we had asked out of courtesy to be present, introduced into the wound a finger which seemed to our excited senses to be about nine inches long, and hooked out the stone at the end of it. "It's always well to bring one in your waistcoat-pocket," said he with a chuckle, "but I suppose you youngsters are above all that."

We made him president of our branch of the British Medical Association, but he resigned after the first meeting. "The young men are too much for me," he said. "I don't understand what they are talking about." Yet his patients do very well. He has the healing touch—that magnetic thing which defies explanation or analysis, but which is a very evident fact none the less. His mere presence leaves the patient with more hopefulness and vitality. The sight of disease affects him as dust does a careful housewife. It makes him angry and impatient. "Tut, tut, this will never do!" he cries, as he takes over a new case. He would shoo Death out of the room as though he were an intrusive hen. But when the intruder refuses to be dislodged, when the blood moves more slowly and the eyes grow dimmer, then it is that Dr. Winter is of more avail than all the drugs in his surgery. Dying folk cling to his hand as if the presence of his bulk and vigour gives them more courage to face the change; and that kindly, windbeaten face has been the last earthly impression which many a sufferer has carried into the unknown.

When Dr. Patterson and I—both of us young, energetic, and up-to-date—settled in the district, we were most cordially received by the old doctor, who would have been only too happy to be relieved of some of his patients. The patients themselves, however, followed their own inclinations—which is a reprehensible way that patients have—so that we remained neglected, with our modern instruments and our latest alkaloids, while he was serving out senna and calomel to all the countryside. We both of us loved the old fellow, but at the same time, in the privacy of our own intimate conversations, we could not help commenting upon this deplorable lack of judgment. "It's all very well for the poorer people," said Patterson. "But after all the educated classes have a right to expect that their medical man will know the difference between a mitral murmur and a bronchitic rale. It's the judicial frame of mind, not the sympathetic, which is the essential one."

I thoroughly agreed with Patterson in what he said. It happened, however, that very shortly afterwards the epidemic of influenza broke out, and we were all worked to death. One morning I met Patterson on my round, and found him looking rather pale and fagged out. He made the same remark about me. I was, in fact, feeling far from well, and I lay upon the sofa all the afternoon with a splitting headache and pains in every joint. As evening closed in, I could no longer disguise the fact that the scourge was upon me, and I felt that I should have medical advice without delay. It was of Patterson, naturally, that I thought, but somehow the idea of him had suddenly become repugnant to me. I thought of his cold, critical attitude, of his endless questions, of his tests and his tappings. I wanted something more soothing—something more genial.

"Mrs. Hudson," said I to my housekeeper, "would you kindly run along to old Dr. Winter and tell him that I should be obliged to him if he would step round?"

She was back with an answer presently. "Dr. Winter will come round in an hour or so, sir; but he has just been called in to attend Dr. Patterson."

HIS FIRST OPERATION.

It was the first day of the winter session, and the third year's man was walking with the first year's man. Twelve o'clock was just booming out from the Tron Church.

"Let me see," said the third year's man. "You have never seen an operation?"

"Never."

"Then this way, please. This is Rutherford's historic bar. A glass of sherry, please, for this gentleman. You are rather sensitive, are you not?"

"My nerves are not very strong, I am afraid."

"Hum! Another glass of sherry for this gentleman. We are going to an operation now, you know."

The novice squared his shoulders and made a gallant attempt to look unconcerned.

"Nothing very bad—eh?"

"Well, yes—pretty bad."

"An—an amputation?"

"No; it's a bigger affair than that."

"I think—I think they must be expecting me at home."

"There's no sense in funking. If you don't go to-day, you must to-morrow. Better get it over at once. Feel pretty fit?"

"Oh, yes; all right!" The smile was not a success.

"One more glass of sherry, then. Now come on or we shall be late. I want you to be well in front."

"Surely that is not necessary."

"Oh, it is far better! What a drove of students! There are plenty of new men among them. You can tell them easily enough, can't you? If they were going down to be operated upon themselves, they could not look whiter."

"I don't think I should look as white."

"Well, I was just the same myself. But the feeling soon wears off. You see a fellow with a face like plaster, and before the week is out he is eating his lunch in the dissecting rooms. I'll tell you all about the case when we get to the theatre."

The students were pouring down the sloping street which led to the infirmary —each with his little sheaf of note-books in his hand. There were pale, frightened lads, fresh from the high schools, and callous old chronics, whose generation had passed on and left them. They swept in an unbroken, tumultuous stream from the university gate to the hospital. The figures and gait of the men were young, but there was little youth in most of their faces. Some looked as if they ate too little—a few as if they drank too much. Tall and short, tweed-coated and black, round-shouldered, bespectacled, and slim, they crowded with clatter of feet and rattle of sticks through the hospital gate. Now and again they thickened into two lines, as the carriage of a surgeon of the staff rolled over the cobblestones between.

"There's going to be a crowd at Archer's," whispered the senior man with suppressed excitement. "It is grand to see him at work. I've seen him jab all round the aorta until it made me jumpy to watch him. This way, and mind the whitewash."

They passed under an archway and down a long, stone-flagged corridor, with drab-coloured doors on either side, each marked with a number. Some of them were ajar, and the novice glanced into them with tingling nerves. He was reassured to catch a glimpse of cheery fires, lines of white-counterpaned beds, and a profusion of coloured texts upon the wall. The corridor opened upon a small hall, with a fringe of poorly clad people seated all round upon benches. A young man, with a pair of scissors stuck like a flower in his buttonhole and a note-book in his hand, was passing from one to the other, whispering and writing.

"Anything good?" asked the third year's man.

"You should have been here yesterday," said the out-patient clerk, glancing up. "We had a regular field day. A popliteal aneurism, a Colles' fracture, a spina bifida, a tropical abscess, and an elephantiasis. How's that for a single haul?"

"I'm sorry I missed it. But they'll come again, I suppose. What's up with the old gentleman?"

A broken workman was sitting in the shadow, rocking himself slowly to and fro, and groaning. A woman beside him was trying to console him, patting his shoulder with a hand which was spotted over with curious little white blisters.

"It's a fine carbuncle," said the clerk, with the air of a connoisseur who describes his orchids to one who can appreciate them. "It's on his back and the passage is draughty, so we must not look at it, must we, daddy? Pemphigus," he added carelessly, pointing to the woman's disfigured hands. "Would you care to stop and take out a metacarpal?"

"No, thank you. We are due at Archer's. Come on!" and they rejoined the throng which was hurrying to the theatre of the famous surgeon.

The tiers of horseshoe benches rising from the floor to the ceiling were already packed, and the novice as he entered saw vague curving lines of faces in front of him, and heard the deep buzz of a hundred voices, and sounds of laughter from somewhere up above him. His companion spied an opening on the second bench, and they both squeezed into it.

"This is grand!" the senior man whispered. "You'll have a rare view of it all."

Only a single row of heads intervened between them and the operating table. It was of unpainted deal, plain, strong, and scrupulously clean. A sheet of brown water-proofing covered half of it, and beneath stood a large tin tray full of sawdust. On the further side, in front of the window, there was a board which was strewed with glittering instruments—forceps, tenacula, saws, canulas, and trocars. A line of knives, with long, thin, delicate blades, lay at one side. Two young men lounged in front of this, one threading needles, the other doing something to a brass coffee-pot-like thing which hissed out puffs of steam.

"That's Peterson," whispered the senior, "the big, bald man in the front row. He's the skin-grafting man, you know. And that's Anthony Browne, who took a larynx out successfully last winter. And there's Murphy, the pathologist, and Stoddart, the eye-man. You'll come to know them all soon."

"Who are the two men at the table?"

"Nobody—dressers. One has charge of the instruments and the other of the puffing Billy. It's Lister's antiseptic spray, you know, and Archer's one of the carbolic-acid men. Hayes is the leader of the cleanliness-and-cold-water school, and they all hate each other like poison."

A flutter of interest passed through the closely packed benches as a woman in petticoat and bodice was led in by two nurses. A red woolen shawl was draped over her head and round her neck. The face which looked out from it was that of a woman in the prime of her years, but drawn with suffering, and of a peculiar beeswax tint. Her head drooped as she walked, and one of the nurses, with her arm round her waist, was whispering consolation in her ear. She gave a quick side-glance at the instrument table as she passed, but the nurses turned her away from it.

"What ails her?" asked the novice.

"Cancer of the parotid. It's the devil of a case; extends right away back behind the carotids. There's hardly a man but Archer would dare to follow it. Ah, here he is himself!"

As he spoke, a small, brisk, iron-grey man came striding into the room, rubbing his hands together as he walked. He had a clean-shaven face, of the naval officer type, with large, bright eyes, and a firm, straight mouth. Behind him came his big house-surgeon, with his gleaming pince-nez, and a trail of dressers, who grouped themselves into the corners of the room.

"Gentlemen," cried the surgeon in a voice as hard and brisk as his manner, "we have here an interesting case of tumour of the parotid, originally cartilaginous but now assuming malignant characteristics, and therefore requiring excision. On to the table, nurse! Thank you! Chloroform, clerk! Thank you! You can take the shawl off, nurse."

The woman lay back upon the water-proofed pillow, and her murderous tumour lay revealed. In itself it was a pretty thing—ivory white, with a mesh of blue veins, and curving gently from jaw to chest. But the lean, yellow face and the stringy throat were in horrible contrast with the plumpness and sleekness of this monstrous growth. The surgeon placed a hand on each side of it and pressed it slowly backwards and forwards.

"Adherent at one place, gentlemen," he cried. "The growth involves the carotids and jugulars, and passes behind the ramus of the jaw, whither we must be prepared to follow it. It is impossible to say how deep our dissection may carry us. Carbolic tray. Thank you! Dressings of carbolic gauze, if you please! Push the chloroform, Mr. Johnson. Have the small saw ready in case it is necessary to remove the jaw."

The patient was moaning gently under the towel which had been placed over her face. She tried to raise her arms and to draw up her knees, but two dressers restrained her. The heavy air was full of the penetrating smells of carbolic acid and of chloroform. A muffled cry came from under the towel, and then a snatch of a song, sung in a high, quavering, monotonous voice:

"He says, says he,
If you fly with me
You'll be mistress of the ice-cream van.
You'll be mistress of the———"

It mumbled off into a drone and stopped. The surgeon came across, still rubbing his hands, and spoke to an elderly man in front of the novice.

"Narrow squeak for the Government," he said.

"Oh, ten is enough."

"They won't have ten long. They'd do better to resign before they are driven to it."

"Oh, I should fight it out."

"What's the use. They can't get past the committee even if they got a vote in the House. I was talking to———"

"Patient's ready, sir," said the dresser.

"Talking to McDonald—but I'll tell you about it presently." He walked back to the patient, who was breathing in long, heavy gasps. "I propose," said he, passing his hand over the tumour in an almost caressing fashion, "to make a free incision over the posterior border, and to take another forward at right angles to the lower end of it. Might I trouble you for a medium knife, Mr. Johnson?"

The novice, with eyes which were dilating with horror, saw the surgeon pick up the long, gleaming knife, dip it into a tin basin, and balance it in his fingers as an artist might his brush. Then he saw him pinch up the skin above the tumour with his left hand. At the sight his nerves, which had already been tried once or twice that day, gave way utterly. His head swain round, and he felt that in another instant he might faint. He dared not look at the patient. He dug his thumbs into his ears lest some scream should come to haunt him, and he fixed his eyes rigidly upon the wooden ledge in front of him. One glance, one cry, would, he knew, break down the shred of self-possession which he still retained. He tried to think of cricket, of green fields and rippling water, of his sisters at home—of anything rather than of what was going on so near him.

And yet somehow, even with his ears stopped up, sounds seemed to penetrate to him and to carry their own tale. He heard, or thought that he heard, the long hissing of the carbolic engine. Then he was conscious of some movement among the dressers. Were there groans, too, breaking in upon him, and some other sound, some fluid sound, which was more dreadfully suggestive still? His mind would keep building up every step of the operation, and fancy made it more ghastly than fact could have been. His nerves tingled and quivered. Minute by minute the giddiness grew more marked, the numb, sickly feeling at his heart more distressing. And then suddenly, with a groan, his head pitching forward, and his brow cracking sharply upon the narrow wooden shelf in front of him, he lay in a dead faint.

When he came to himself, he was lying in the empty theatre, with his collar and shirt undone. The third year's man was dabbing a wet sponge over his face, and a couple of grinning dressers were looking on.

"All right," cried the novice, sitting up and rubbing his eyes. "I'm sorry to have made an ass of myself."

"Well, so I should think," said his companion.

"What on earth did you faint about?"

"I couldn't help it. It was that operation."

"What operation?"

"Why, that cancer."

There was a pause, and then the three students burst out laughing. "Why, you juggins!" cried the senior man, "there never was an operation at all! They found the patient didn't stand the chloroform well, and so the whole thing was off. Archer has been giving us one of his racy lectures, and you fainted just in the middle of his favourite story."

A STRAGGLER OF '15.

It was a dull October morning, and heavy, rolling fog-wreaths lay low over the wet grey roofs of the Woolwich houses. Down in the long, brick-lined streets all was sodden and greasy and cheerless. From the high dark buildings of the arsenal came the whirr of many wheels, the thudding of weights, and the buzz and babel of human toil. Beyond, the dwellings of the workingmen, smoke-stained and unlovely, radiated away in a lessening perspective of narrowing road and dwindling wall.

There were few folk in the streets, for the toilers had all been absorbed since break of day by the huge smoke-spouting monster, which sucked in the manhood of the town, to belch it forth weary and work-stained every night. Little groups of children straggled to school, or loitered to peep through the single, front windows at the big, gilt-edged Bibles, balanced upon small, three-legged tables, which were their usual adornment. Stout women, with thick, red arms and dirty aprons, stood upon the whitened doorsteps, leaning upon their brooms, and shrieking their morning greetings across the road. One stouter, redder, and dirtier than the rest, had gathered a small knot of cronies around her and was talking energetically, with little shrill titters from her audience to punctuate her remarks.

"Old enough to know better!" she cried, in answer to an exclamation from one of the listeners. "If he hain't no sense now, I 'specs he won't learn much on this side o' Jordan. Why, 'ow old is he at all? Blessed if I could ever make out."

"Well, it ain't so hard to reckon," said a sharp-featured pale-faced woman with watery blue eyes. "He's been at the battle o' Waterloo, and has the pension and medal to prove it."

"That were a ter'ble long time agone," remarked a third. "It were afore I were born."

"It were fifteen year after the beginnin' of the century," cried a younger woman, who had stood leaning against the wall, with a smile of superior knowledge upon her face. "My Bill was a-saying so last Sabbath, when I spoke to him o' old Daddy Brewster, here."

"And suppose he spoke truth, Missus Simpson, 'ow long agone do that make it?"

"It's eighty-one now," said the original speaker, checking off the years upon her coarse red fingers, "and that were fifteen. Ten and ten, and ten, and ten, and ten—why, it's only sixty-and-six year, so he ain't so old after all."

"But he weren't a newborn babe at the battle, silly!" cried the young woman with a chuckle. "S'pose he were only twenty, then he couldn't be less than six-and-eighty now, at the lowest."

"Aye, he's that—every day of it," cried several.

"I've had 'bout enough of it," remarked the large woman gloomily. "Unless his young niece, or grandniece, or whatever she is, come to-day, I'm off, and he can find some one else to do his work. Your own 'ome first, says I."

"Ain't he quiet, then, Missus Simpson?" asked the youngest of the group.

"Listen to him now," she answered, with her hand half raised and her head turned slantwise towards the open door. From the upper floor there came a shuffling, sliding sound with a sharp tapping of a stick. "There he go back and forrards, doing what he call his sentry go. 'Arf the night through he's at that game, the silly old juggins. At six o'clock this very mornin there he was beatin' with a stick at my door. 'Turn out, guard!' he cried, and a lot more jargon that I could make nothing of. Then what with his coughin' and 'awkin' and spittin', there ain't no gettin' a wink o' sleep. Hark to him now!"

"Missus Simpson, Missus Simpson!" cried a cracked and querulous voice from above.

"That's him!" she cried, nodding her head with an air of triumph. "He do go on somethin' scandalous. Yes, Mr. Brewster, sir."

"I want my morning ration, Missus Simpson."

"It's just ready, Mr. Brewster, sir."

"Blessed if he ain't like a baby cryin' for its pap," said the young woman.

"I feel as if I could shake his old bones up sometimes!" cried Mrs. Simpson viciously. "But who's for a 'arf of fourpenny?"

The whole company were about to shuffle off to the public house, when a young girl stepped across the road and touched the housekeeper timidly upon the arm. "I think that is No. 56 Arsenal View," she said. "Can you tell me if Mr. Brewster lives here?"

The housekeeper looked critically at the newcomer. She was a girl of about twenty, broad-faced and comely, with a turned-up nose and large, honest grey eyes. Her print dress, her straw hat, with its bunch of glaring poppies, and the bundle she carried, had all a smack of the country.

"You're Norah Brewster, I s'pose," said Mrs. Simpson, eyeing her up and down with no friendly gaze.

"Yes, I've come to look after my Granduncle Gregory."

"And a good job too," cried the housekeeper, with a toss of her head. "It's about time that some of his own folk took a turn at it, for I've had enough of it. There you are, young woman! In you go and make yourself at home. There's tea in the caddy and bacon on the dresser, and the old man will be about you if you don't fetch him his breakfast. I'll send for my things in the evenin'." With a nod she strolled off with her attendant gossips in the direction of the public house.

Thus left to her own devices, the country girl walked into the front room and took off her hat and jacket. It was a low-roofed apartment with a sputtering fire upon which a small brass kettle was singing cheerily. A stained cloth lay over half the table, with an empty brown teapot, a loaf of bread, and some coarse crockery. Norah Brewster looked rapidly about her, and in an instant took over her new duties. Ere five minutes had passed the tea was made, two slices of bacon were frizzling on the pan, the table was rearranged, the antimacassars straightened over the sombre brown furniture, and the whole room had taken a new air of comfort and neatness. This done she looked round curiously at the prints upon the walls. Over the fireplace, in a small, square case, a brown medal caught her eye, hanging from a strip of purple ribbon. Beneath was a slip of newspaper cutting. She stood on her tiptoes, with her fingers on the edge of the mantelpiece, and craned her neck up to see it, glancing down from time to time at the bacon which simmered and hissed beneath her. The cutting was yellow with age, and ran in this way:

"On Tuesday an interesting ceremony was performed at the barracks of the Third Regiment of Guards, when, in the presence of the Prince Regent, Lord Hill, Lord Saltoun, and an assemblage which comprised beauty as well as valour, a special medal was presented to Corporal Gregory Brewster, of Captain Haldane's flank company, in recognition of his gallantry in the recent great battle in the Lowlands. It appears that on the ever-memorable 18th of June four companies of the Third Guards and of the Coldstreams, under the command of Colonels Maitland and Byng, held the important farmhouse of Hougoumont at the right of the British position. At a critical point of the action these troops found themselves short of powder. Seeing that Generals Foy and Jerome Buonaparte were again massing their infantry for an attack on the position, Colonel Byng dispatched Corporal Brewster to the rear to hasten up the reserve ammunition. Brewster came upon two powder tumbrils of the Nassau division, and succeeded, after menacing the drivers with his musket, in inducing them to convey their powder to Hougoumont. In his absence, however, the hedges surrounding the position had been set on fire by a howitzer battery of the French, and the passage of the carts full of powder became a most hazardous matter. The first tumbril exploded, blowing the driver to fragments. Daunted by the fate of his comrade, the second driver turned his horses, but Corporal Brewster, springing upon his seat, hurled the man down, and urging the powder cart through the flames, succeeded in forcing his way to his companions. To this gallant deed may be directly attributed the success of the British arms, for without powder it would have been impossible to have held Hougoumont, and the Duke of Wellington had repeatedly declared that had Hougoumont fallen, as well as La Haye Sainte, he would have found it impossible to have held his ground. Long may the heroic Brewster live to treasure the medal which he has so bravely won, and to look back with pride to the day when, in the presence of his comrades, he received this tribute to his valour from the august hands of the first gentleman of the realm."

The reading of this old cutting increased in the girl's mind the veneration which she had always had for her warrior kinsman. From her infancy he had been her hero, and she remembered how her father used to speak of his courage and his strength, how he could strike down a bullock with a blow of his fist and carry a fat sheep under either arm. True, she had never seen him, but a rude painting at home which depicted a square-faced, clean shaven, stalwart man with a great bearskin cap, rose ever before her memory when she thought of him.

She was still gazing at the brown medal and wondering what the "Dulce et decorum est" might mean, which was inscribed upon the edge, when there came a sudden tapping and shuffling upon the stair, and there at the door was standing the very man who had been so often in her thoughts.

But could this indeed be he? Where was the martial air, the flashing eye, the warrior face which she had pictured? There, framed in the doorway, was a huge twisted old man, gaunt and puckered, with twitching hands and shuffling, purposeless feet. A cloud of fluffy white hair, a red-veined nose, two thick tufts of eyebrow and a pair of dimly questioning, watery blue eyes—these were what met her gaze. He leaned forward upon a stick, while his shoulders rose and fell with his crackling, rasping breathing.

"I want my morning rations," he crooned, as he stumped forward to his chair. "The cold nips me without 'em. See to my fingers!" He held out his distorted hands, all blue at the tips, wrinkled and gnarled, with huge, projecting knuckles.

"It's nigh ready," answered the girl, gazing at him with wonder in her eyes. "Don't you know who I am, granduncle? I am Norah Brewster from Witham."

"Rum is warm," mumbled the old man, rocking to and fro in his chair, "and schnapps is warm, and there's 'eat in soup, but it's a dish o' tea for me. What did you say your name was?"

"Norah Brewster."

"You can speak out, lass. Seems to me folk's voices isn't as loud as they used."

"I'm Norah Brewster, uncle. I'm your grandniece come down from Essex way to live with you."

"You'll be brother Jarge's girl! Lor, to think o' little Jarge having a girl!" He chuckled hoarsely to himself, and the long, stringy sinews of his throat jerked and quivered.

"I am the daughter of your brother George's son," said she, as she turned the bacon.

"Lor, but little Jarge was a rare un!" he continued. "Eh, by Jimini, there was no chousing Jarge. He's got a bull pup o' mine that I gave him when I took the bounty. You've heard him speak of it, likely?"

"Why, grandpa George has been dead this twenty year," said she, pouring out the tea.

"Well, it was a bootiful pup—aye, a well-bred un, by Jimini! I'm cold for lack o' my rations. Rum is good, and so is schnapps, but I'd as lief have tea as either."

He breathed heavily while he devoured his food. "It's a middlin' goodish way you've come," said he at last. "Likely the stage left yesternight."

"The what, uncle?"

"The coach that brought you."

"Nay, I came by the mornin' train."

"Lor, now, think o' that! You ain't afeard o' those newfangled things! By Jimini, to think of you comin' by railroad like that! What's the world a-comin' to!"

There was silence for some minutes while Norah sat stirring her tea and glancing sideways at the bluish lips and champing jaws of her companion.

"You must have seen a deal o' life, uncle," said she. "It must seem a long, long time to you!"

"Not so very long neither. I'm ninety, come Candlemas; but it don't seem long since I took the bounty. And that battle, it might have been yesterday. Eh, but I get a power o' good from my rations!" He did indeed look less worn and colourless than when she first saw him. His face was flushed and his back more erect.

"Have you read that?" he asked, jerking his head towards the cutting.

"Yes, uncle, and I'm sure you must be proud of it."

"Ah, it was a great day for me! A great day! The Regent was there, and a fine body of a man too! 'The ridgment is proud of you,' says he. 'And I'm proud of the ridgment,' say I. 'A damned good answer too!' says he to Lord Hill, and they both bu'st out a-laughin'. But what be you a-peepin' out o' the window for?"

"Oh, uncle, here's a regiment of soldiers coming down the street with the band playing in front of them."

"A ridgment, eh? Where be my glasses? Lor, but I can hear the band, as plain as plain! Here's the pioneers an' the drum-major! What be their number, lass?" His eyes were shining and his bony yellow fingers, like the claws of some fierce old bird, dug into her shoulder.

"They don't seem to have no number, uncle. They've something wrote on their shoulders. Oxfordshire, I think it be."

"Ah, yes!" he growled. "I heard as they'd dropped the numbers and given them newfangled names. There they go, by Jimini! They're young mostly, but they hain't forgot how to march. They have the swing-aye, I'll say that for them. They've got the swing." He gazed after them until the last files had turned the corner and the measured tramp of their marching had died away in the distance.

He had just regained his chair when the door opened and a gentleman stepped in.

"Ah, Mr. Brewster! Better to-day?" he asked.

"Come in, doctor! Yes, I'm better. But there's a deal o' bubbling in my chest. It's all them toobes. If I could but cut the phlegm, I'd be right. Can't you give me something to cut the phlegm?"

The doctor, a grave-faced young man, put his fingers to the furrowed, blue-corded wrist.

"You must be careful," he said. "You must take no liberties." The thin tide of life seemed to thrill rather than to throb under his finger.

The old man chuckled.

"I've got brother Jarge's girl to look after me now. She'll see I don't break barracks or do what I hadn't ought to. Why, darn my skin, I knew something was amiss!"

"With what?"

"Why, with them soldiers. You saw them pass, doctor—eh? They'd forgot their stocks. Not one on 'em had his stock on." He croaked and chuckled for a long time over his discovery. "It wouldn't ha' done for the Dook!" he muttered. "No, by Jimini! the Dook would ha' had a word there."

The doctor smiled. "Well, you are doing very well," said he. "I'll look in once a week or so, and see how you are." As Norah followed him to the door, he beckoned her outside.

"He is very weak," he whispered. "If you find him failing you must send for me."

"What ails him, doctor?"

"Ninety years ails him. His arteries are pipes of lime. His heart is shrunken and flabby. The man is worn out."

Norah stood watching the brisk figure of the young doctor, and pondering over these new responsibilities which had come upon her. When she turned a tall, brown-faced artilleryman, with the three gold chevrons of sergeant upon his arm, was standing, carbine in hand, at her elbow.

"Good-morning, miss," said he, raising one thick finger to his jaunty, yellow-banded cap. "I b'lieve there's an old gentleman lives here of the name of Brewster, who was engaged in the battle o' Waterloo?"

"It's my granduncle, sir," said Norah, casting down her eyes before the keen, critical gaze of the young soldier. "He is in the front parlour."

"Could I have a word with him, miss? I'll call again if it don't chance to be convenient."

"I am sure that he would be very glad to see you, sir. He's in here, if you'll step in. Uncle, here's a gentleman who wants to speak with you."

"Proud to see you, sir—proud and glad, sir," cried the sergeant, taking three steps forward into the room, and grounding his carbine while he raised his hand, palm forwards, in a salute. Norah stood by the door, with her mouth and eyes open, wondering if her granduncle had ever, in his prime, looked like this magnificent creature, and whether he, in his turn, would ever come to resemble her granduncle.

The old man blinked up at his visitor, and shook his head slowly. "Sit ye down, sergeant," said he, pointing with his stick to a chair. "You're full young for the stripes. Lordy, it's easier to get three now than one in my day. Gunners were old soldiers then and the grey hairs came quicker than the three stripes."

"I am eight years' service, sir," cried the sergeant. "Macdonald is my name—Sergeant Macdonald, of H Battery, Southern Artillery Division. I have called as the spokesman of my mates at the gunner's barracks to say that we are proud to have you in the town, sir."

Old Brewster chuckled and rubbed his bony hands. "That were what the Regent said," he cried. "'The ridgment is proud of ye,' says he. 'And I am proud of the ridgment,' says I. 'And a damned good answer too,' says he, and he and Lord Hill bu'st out a-laughin'."

"The non-commissioned mess would be proud and honoured to see you, sir," said Sergeant Macdonald; "and if you could step as far you'll always find a pipe o' baccy and a glass o' grog a-waitin' you."

The old man laughed until he coughed. "Like to see me, would they? The dogs!" said he. "Well, well, when the warm weather comes again I'll maybe drop in. Too grand for a canteen, eh? Got your mess just the same as the orficers. What's the world a-comin' to at all!"

"You was in the line, sir, was you not?" asked the sergeant respectfully.

"The line?" cried the old man, with shrill scorn. "Never wore a shako in my life. I am a guardsman, I am. Served in the Third Guards—the same they call now the Scots Guards. Lordy, but they have all marched away—every man of them—from old Colonel Byng down to the drummer boys, and here am I a straggler—that's what I am, sergeant, a straggler! I'm here when I ought to be there. But it ain't my fault neither, for I'm ready to fall in when the word comes."

"We've all got to muster there," answered the sergeant. "Won't you try my baccy, sir?" handing over a sealskin pouch.

Old Brewster drew a blackened clay pipe from his pocket, and began to stuff the tobacco into the bowl. In an instant it slipped through his fingers, and was broken to pieces on the floor. His lip quivered, his nose puckered up, and he began crying with the long, helpless sobs of a child. "I've broke my pipe," he cried.

"Don't, uncle; oh, don't!" cried Norah, bending over him, and patting his white head as one soothes a baby. "It don't matter. We can easy get another."

"Don't you fret yourself, sir," said the sergeant. "'Ere's a wooden pipe with an amber mouth, if you'll do me the honour to accept it from me. I'd be real glad if you will take it."

"Jimini!" cried he, his smiles breaking in an instant through his tears. "It's a fine pipe. See to my new pipe, Norah. I lay that Jarge never had a pipe like that. You've got your firelock there, sergeant?"

"Yes, sir. I was on my way back from the butts when I looked in."

"Let me have the feel of it. Lordy, but it seems like old times to have one's hand on a musket. What's the manual, sergeant, eh? Cock your firelock—look to your priming—present your firelock—eh, sergeant? Oh, Jimini, I've broke your musket in halves!"

"That's all right, sir," cried the gunner laughing. "You pressed on the lever and opened the breech-piece. That's where we load 'em, you know."

"Load 'em at the wrong end! Well, well, to think o' that! And no ramrod neither! I've heard tell of it, but I never believed it afore. Ah! it won't come up to brown Bess. When there's work to be done, you mark my word and see if they don't come back to brown Bess."

"By the Lord, sir!" cried the sergeant hotly, "they need some change out in South Africa now. I see by this mornin's paper that the Government has knuckled under to these Boers. They're hot about it at the non-com. mess, I can tell you, sir."

"Eh—eh," croaked old Brewster. "By Jimini! it wouldn't ha' done for the Dook; the Dook would ha' had a word to say over that."

"Ah, that he would, sir!" cried the sergeant; "and God send us another like him. But I've wearied you enough for one sitting. I'll look in again, and I'll bring a comrade or two with me, if I may, for there isn't one but would be proud to have speech with you."

So, with another salute to the veteran and a gleam of white teeth at Norah, the big gunner withdrew, leaving a memory of blue cloth and of gold braid behind him. Many days had not passed, however, before he was back again, and during all the long winter he was a frequent visitor at Arsenal View. There came a time, at last, when it might be doubted to which of the two occupants his visits were directed, nor was it hard to say by which he was most anxiously awaited. He brought others with him; and soon, through all the lines, a pilgrimage to Daddy Brewster's came to be looked upon as the proper thing to do. Gunners and sappers, linesmen and dragoons, came bowing and bobbing into the little parlour, with clatter of side arms and clink of spurs, stretching their long legs across the patchwork rug, and hunting in the front of their tunics for the screw of tobacco or paper of snuff which they had brought as a sign of their esteem.

It was a deadly cold winter, with six weeks on end of snow on the ground, and Norah had a hard task to keep the life in that time-worn body. There were times when his mind would leave him, and when, save an animal outcry when the hour of his meals came round, no word would fall from him. He was a white-haired child, with all a child's troubles and emotions. As the warm weather came once more, however, and the green buds peeped forth again upon the trees, the blood thawed in his veins, and he would even drag himself as far as the door to bask in the life-giving sunshine.

"It do hearten me up so," he said one morning, as he glowed in the hot May sun. "It's a job to keep back the flies, though. They get owdacious in this weather, and they do plague me cruel."

"I'll keep them off you, uncle," said Norah.

"Eh, but it's fine! This sunshine makes me think o' the glory to come. You might read me a bit o' the Bible, lass. I find it wonderful soothing."

"What part would you like, uncle?"

"Oh, them wars."

"The wars?"

"Aye, keep to the wars! Give me the Old Testament for choice. There's more taste to it, to my mind. When parson comes he wants to get off to something else; but it's Joshua or nothing with me. Them Israelites was good soldiers—good growed soldiers, all of 'em."

"But, uncle," pleaded Norah, "it's all peace in the next world."

"No, it ain't, gal."

"Oh, yes, uncle, surely!"

The old corporal knocked his stick irritably upon the ground. "I tell ye it ain't, gal. I asked parson."

"Well, what did he say?"

"He said there was to be a last fight. He even gave it a name, he did. The battle of Arm—Arm——"

"Armageddon."

"Aye, that's the name parson said. I 'specs the Third Guards'll be there. And the Dook—the Dook'll have a word to say."

An elderly, grey-whiskered gentleman had been walking down the street, glancing up at the numbers of the houses. Now as his eyes fell upon the old man, he came straight for him.

"Hullo!" said he; "perhaps you are Gregory Brewster?"

"My name, sir," answered the veteran.

"You are the same Brewster, as I understand, who is on the roll of the Scots Guards as having been present at the battle of Waterloo?"

"I am that man, sir, though we called it the Third Guards in those days. It was a fine ridgment, and they only need me to make up a full muster."

"Tut, tut! they'll have to wait years for that," said the gentleman heartily. "But I am the colonel of the Scots Guards, and I thought I would like to have a word with you."

Old Gregory Brewster was up in an instant, with his hand to his rabbit-skin cap. "God bless me!" he cried, "to think of it! to think of it!"

"Hadn't the gentleman better come in?" suggested the practical Norah from behind the door.

"Surely, sir, surely; walk in, sir, if I may be so bold." In his excitement he had forgotten his stick, and as he led the way into the parlour his knees tottered, and he threw out his hands. In an instant the colonel had caught him on one side and Norah on the other.

"Easy and steady," said the colonel, as he led him to his armchair.

"Thank ye, sir; I was near gone that time. But, Lordy I why, I can scarce believe it. To think of me the corporal of the flank company and you the colonel of the battalion! How things come round, to be sure!"

"Why, we are very proud of you in London," said the colonel. "And so you are actually one of the men who held Hougoumont." He looked at the bony, trembling hands, with their huge, knotted knuckles, the stringy throat, and the heaving, rounded shoulders. Could this, indeed, be the last of that band of heroes? Then he glanced at the half-filled phials, the blue liniment bottles, the long-spouted kettle, and the sordid details of the sick room. "Better, surely, had he died under the blazing rafters of the Belgian farmhouse," thought the colonel.

"I hope that you are pretty comfortable and happy," he remarked after a pause.

"Thank ye, sir. I have a good deal o' trouble with my toobes—a deal o' trouble. You wouldn't think the job it is to cut the phlegm. And I need my rations. I gets cold without 'em. And the flies! I ain't strong enough to fight against them."

"How's the memory?" asked the colonel.

"Oh, there ain't nothing amiss there. Why, sir, I could give you the name of every man in Captain Haldane's flank company."

"And the battle—you remember it?"

"Why, I sees it all afore me every time I shuts my eyes. Lordy, sir, you wouldn't hardly believe how clear it is to me. There's our line from the paregoric bottle right along to the snuff box. D'ye see? Well, then, the pill box is for Hougoumont on the right—where we was—and Norah's thimble for La Haye Sainte. There it is, all right, sir; and here were our guns, and here behind the reserves and the Belgians. Ach, them Belgians!" He spat furiously into the fire. "Then here's the French, where my pipe lies; and over here, where I put my baccy pouch, was the Proosians a-comin' up on our left flank. Jimini, but it was a glad sight to see the smoke of their guns!"

"And what was it that struck you most now in connection with the whole affair?" asked the colonel.

"I lost three half-crowns over it, I did," crooned old Brewster. "I shouldn't wonder if I was never to get that money now. I lent 'em to Jabez Smith, my rear rank man, in Brussels. 'Only till pay-day, Grig,' says he. By Gosh! he was stuck by a lancer at Quatre Bras, and me with not so much as a slip o' paper to prove the debt! Them three half-crowns is as good as lost to me."

The colonel rose from his chair laughing. "The officers of the Guards want you to buy yourself some little trifle which may add to your comfort," he said. "It is not from me, so you need not thank me." He took up the old man's tobacco pouch and slipped a crisp banknote inside it.

"Thank ye kindly, sir. But there's one favour that I would like to ask you, colonel."

"Yes, my man."

"If I'm called, colonel, you won't grudge me a flag and a firing party? I'm not a civilian; I'm a guardsman—I'm the last of the old Third Guards."

"All right, my man, I'll see to it," said the colonel. "Good-bye; I hope to have nothing but good news from you."

"A kind gentleman, Norah," croaked old Brewster, as they saw him walk past the window; "but, Lordy, he ain't fit to hold the stirrup o' my Colonel Byng!"

It was on the very next day that the old corporal took a sudden change for the worse. Even the golden sunlight streaming through the window seemed unable to warm that withered frame. The doctor came and shook his head in silence.

All day the man lay with only his puffing blue lips and the twitching of his scraggy neck to show that he still held the breath of life. Norah and Sergeant Macdonald had sat by him in the afternoon, but he had shown no consciousness of their presence. He lay peacefully, his eyes half closed, his hands under his cheek, as one who is very weary.

They had left him for an instant and were sitting in the front room, where Norah was preparing tea, when of a sudden they heard a shout that rang through the house. Loud and clear and swelling, it pealed in their ears—a voice full of strength and energy and fiery passion. "The Guards need powder!" it cried; and yet again, "The Guards need powder!"

The sergeant sprang from his chair and rushed in, followed by the trembling Norah. There was the old man standing up, his blue eyes sparkling, his white hair bristling, his whole figure towering and expanding, with eagle head and glance of fire. "The Guards need powder!" he thundered once again, "and, by God, they shall have it!" He threw up his long arms, and sank back with a groan into his chair. The sergeant stooped over him, and his face darkened.

"Oh, Archie, Archie," sobbed the frightened girl, "what do you think of him?"

The sergeant turned away. "I think," said he, "that the Third Guards have a full muster now."

THE THIRD GENERATION.

Scudamore Lane, sloping down riverwards from just behind the Monument, lies at night in the shadow of two black and monstrous walls which loom high above the glimmer of the scattered gas lamps. The footpaths are narrow, and the causeway is paved with rounded cobblestones, so that the endless drays roar along it like breaking waves. A few old-fashioned houses lie scattered among the business premises, and in one of these, half-way down on the left-hand side, Dr. Horace Selby conducts his large practice. It is a singular street for so big a man; but a specialist who has an European reputation can afford to live where he likes. In his particular branch, too, patients do not always regard seclusion as a disadvantage.

It was only ten o'clock. The dull roar of the traffic which converged all day upon London Bridge had died away now to a mere confused murmur. It was raining heavily, and the gas shone dimly through the streaked and dripping glass, throwing little circles upon the glistening cobblestones. The air was full of the sounds of the rain, the thin swish of its fall, the heavier drip from the eaves, and the swirl and gurgle down the two steep gutters and through the sewer grating. There was only one figure in the whole length of Scudamore Lane. It was that of a man, and it stood outside the door of Dr. Horace Selby.

He had just rung and was waiting for an answer. The fanlight beat full upon the gleaming shoulders of his waterproof and upon his upturned features. It was a wan, sensitive, clear-cut face, with some subtle, nameless peculiarity in its expression, something of the startled horse in the white-rimmed eye, something too of the helpless child in the drawn cheek and the weakening of the lower lip. The man-servant knew the stranger as a patient at a bare glance at those frightened eyes. Such a look had been seen at that door many times before.

"Is the doctor in?"

The man hesitated.

"He has had a few friends to dinner, sir. He does not like to be disturbed outside his usual hours, sir."

"Tell him that I MUST see him. Tell him that it is of the very first importance. Here is my card." He fumbled with his trembling fingers in trying to draw one from his case. "Sir Francis Norton is the name. Tell him that Sir Francis Norton, of Deane Park, must see him without delay."

"Yes, sir." The butler closed his fingers upon the card and the half-sovereign which accompanied it. "Better hang your coat up here in the hall. It is very wet. Now if you will wait here in the consulting-room, I have no doubt that I shall be able to send the doctor in to you."

It was a large and lofty room in which the young baronet found himself. The carpet was so soft and thick that his feet made no sound as he walked across it. The two gas jets were turned only half-way up, and the dim light with the faint aromatic smell which filled the air had a vaguely religious suggestion. He sat down in a shining leather armchair by the smouldering fire and looked gloomily about him. Two sides of the room were taken up with books, fat and sombre, with broad gold lettering upon their backs. Beside him was the high, old-fashioned mantelpiece of white marble—the top of it strewed with cotton wadding and bandages, graduated measures, and little bottles. There was one with a broad neck just above him containing bluestone, and another narrower one with what looked like the ruins of a broken pipestem and "Caustic" outside upon a red label. Thermometers, hypodermic syringes bistouries and spatulas were scattered about both on the mantelpiece and on the central table on either side of the sloping desk. On the same table, to the right, stood copies of the five books which Dr. Horace Selby had written upon the subject with which his name is peculiarly associated, while on the left, on the top of a red medical directory, lay a huge glass model of a human eye the size of a turnip, which opened down the centre to expose the lens and double chamber within.

Sir Francis Norton had never been remarkable for his powers of observation, and yet he found himself watching these trifles with the keenest attention. Even the corrosion of the cork of an acid bottle caught his eye, and he wondered that the doctor did not use glass stoppers. Tiny scratches where the light glinted off from the table, little stains upon the leather of the desk, chemical formulae scribbled upon the labels of the phials—nothing was too slight to arrest his attention. And his sense of hearing was equally alert. The heavy ticking of the solemn black clock above the mantelpiece struck quite painfully upon his ears. Yet in spite of it, and in spite also of the thick, old-fashioned wooden partition, he could hear voices of men talking in the next room, and could even catch scraps of their conversation. "Second hand was bound to take it." "Why, you drew the last of them yourself!"

"How could I play the queen when I knew that the ace was against me?" The phrases came in little spurts falling back into the dull murmur of conversation. And then suddenly he heard the creaking of a door and a step in the hall, and knew with a tingling mixture of impatience and horror that the crisis of his life was at hand.

Dr. Horace Selby was a large, portly man with an imposing presence. His nose and chin were bold and pronounced, yet his features were puffy, a combination which would blend more freely with the wig and cravat of the early Georges than with the close-cropped hair and black frock-coat of the end of the nineteenth century. He was clean shaven, for his mouth was too good to cover —large, flexible, and sensitive, with a kindly human softening at either corner which with his brown sympathetic eyes had drawn out many a shame-struck sinner's secret. Two masterful little bushy side-whiskers bristled out from under his ears spindling away upwards to merge in the thick curves of his brindled hair. To his patients there was something reassuring in the mere bulk and dignity of the man. A high and easy bearing in medicine as in war bears with it a hint of victories in the past, and a promise of others to come. Dr. Horace Selby's face was a consolation, and so too were the large, white, soothing hands, one of which he held out to his visitor.

"I am sorry to have kept you waiting. It is a conflict of duties, you perceive—a host's to his guests and an adviser's to his patient. But now I am entirely at your disposal, Sir Francis. But dear me, you are very cold."

"Yes, I am cold."

"And you are trembling all over. Tut, tut, this will never do! This miserable night has chilled you. Perhaps some little stimulant——"

"No, thank you. I would really rather not. And it is not the night which has chilled me. I am frightened, doctor."

The doctor half-turned in his chair, and he patted the arch of the young man's knee, as he might the neck of a restless horse.

"What then?" he asked, looking over his shoulder at the pale face with the startled eyes.

Twice the young man parted his lips. Then he stooped with a sudden gesture, and turning up the right leg of his trousers he pulled down his sock and thrust forward his shin. The doctor made a clicking noise with his tongue as he glanced at it.

"Both legs?"

"No, only one."

"Suddenly?"

"This morning."

"Hum."

The doctor pouted his lips, and drew his finger and thumb down the line of his chin. "Can you account for it?" he asked briskly.

"No."

A trace of sternness came into the large brown eyes.

"I need not point out to you that unless the most absolute frankness———"

The patient sprang from his chair. "So help me God!" he cried, "I have nothing in my life with which to reproach myself. Do you think that I would be such a fool as to come here and tell you lies. Once for all, I have nothing to regret." He was a pitiful, half-tragic and half-grotesque figure, as he stood with one trouser leg rolled to the knee, and that ever present horror still lurking in his eyes. A burst of merriment came from the card-players in the next room, and the two looked at each other in silence.

"Sit down," said the doctor abruptly, "your assurance is quite sufficient." He stooped and ran his finger down the line of the young man's shin, raising it at one point. "Hum, serpiginous," he murmured, shaking his head. "Any other symptoms?"

"My eyes have been a little weak."

"Let me see your teeth." He glanced at them, and again made the gentle, clicking sound of sympathy and disapprobation.

"Now your eye." He lit a lamp at the patient's elbow, and holding a small crystal lens to concentrate the light, he threw it obliquely upon the patient's eye. As he did so a glow of pleasure came over his large expressive face, a flush of such enthusiasm as the botanist feels when he packs the rare plant into his tin knapsack, or the astronomer when the long-sought comet first swims into the field of his telescope.

"This is very typical—very typical indeed," he murmured, turning to his desk and jotting down a few memoranda upon a sheet of paper. "Curiously enough, I am writing a monograph upon the subject. It is singular that you should have been able to furnish so well-marked a case." He had so forgotten the patient in his symptom, that he had assumed an almost congratulatory air towards its possessor. He reverted to human sympathy again, as his patient asked for particulars.

"My dear sir, there is no occasion for us to go into strictly professional details together," said he soothingly. "If, for example, I were to say that you have interstitial keratitis, how would you be the wiser? There are indications of a strumous diathesis. In broad terms, I may say that you have a constitutional and hereditary taint."

The young baronet sank back in his chair, and his chin fell forwards upon his chest. The doctor sprang to a side-table and poured out half a glass of liqueur brandy which he held to his patient's lips. A little fleck of colour came into his cheeks as he drank it down.

"Perhaps I spoke a little abruptly," said the doctor, "but you must have known the nature of your complaint. Why, otherwise, should you have come to me?"

"God help me, I suspected it; but only today when my leg grew bad. My father had a leg like this."

"It was from him, then——?"

"No, from my grandfather. You have heard of Sir Rupert Norton, the great Corinthian?"

The doctor was a man of wide reading with a retentive, memory. The name brought back instantly to him the remembrance of the sinister reputation of its owner—a notorious buck of the thirties—who had gambled and duelled and steeped himself in drink and debauchery, until even the vile set with whom he consorted had shrunk away from him in horror, and left him to a sinister old age with the barmaid wife whom he had married in some drunken frolic. As he looked at the young man still leaning back in the leather chair, there seemed for the instant to flicker up behind him some vague presentiment of that foul old dandy with his dangling seals, many-wreathed scarf, and dark satyric face.

What was he now? An armful of bones in a mouldy box. But his deeds— they were living and rotting the blood in the veins of an innocent man.

"I see that you have heard of him," said the young baronet. "He died horribly, I have been told; but not more horribly than he had lived. My father was his only son. He was a studious man, fond of books and canaries and the country; but his innocent life did not save him."

"His symptoms were cutaneous, I understand."

"He wore gloves in the house. That was the first thing I can remember. And then it was his throat. And then his legs. He used to ask me so often about my own health, and I thought him so fussy, for how could I tell what the meaning of it was. He was always watching me—always with a sidelong eye fixed upon me. Now, at last, I know what he was watching for."

"Had you brothers or sisters?"

"None, thank God."

"Well, well, it is a sad case, and very typical of many which come in my way. You are no lonely sufferer, Sir Francis. There are many thousands who bear the same cross as you do."

"But where is the justice of it, doctor?" cried the young man, springing from his chair and pacing up and down the consulting-room. "If I were heir to my grandfather's sins as well as to their results, I could understand it, but I am of my father's type. I love all that is gentle and beautiful—music and poetry and art. The coarse and animal is abhorrent to me. Ask any of my friends and they would tell you that. And now that this vile, loathsome thing—ach, I am polluted to the marrow, soaked in abomination! And why? Haven't I a right to ask why? Did I do it? Was it my fault? Could I help being born? And look at me now, blighted and blasted, just as life was at its sweetest. Talk about the sins of the father—how about the sins of the Creator?" He shook his two clinched hands in the air—the poor impotent atom with his pin-point of brain caught in the whirl of the infinite.

The doctor rose and placing his hands upon his shoulders he pressed him back into his chair once more. "There, there, my dear lad," said he; "you must not excite yourself. You are trembling all over. Your nerves cannot stand it. We must take these great questions upon trust. What are we, after all? Half-evolved creatures in a transition stage, nearer perhaps to the Medusa on the one side than to perfected humanity on the other. With half a complete brain we can't expect to understand the whole of a complete fact, can we, now? It is all very dim and dark, no doubt; but I think that Pope's famous couplet sums up the whole matter, and from my heart, after fifty years of varied experience,

I can say——"

But the young baronet gave a cry of impatience and disgust. "Words, words, words! You can sit comfortably there in your chair and say them—and think them too, no doubt. You've had your life, but I've never had mine. You've healthy blood in your veins; mine is putrid. And yet I am as innocent as you. What would words do for you if you were in this chair and I in that? Ah, it's such a mockery and a make-believe! Don't think me rude, though, doctor. I don't mean to be that. I only say that it is impossible for you or any other man to realise it. But I've a question to ask you, doctor. It's one on which my whole life must depend." He writhed his fingers together in an agony of apprehension.

"Speak out, my dear sir. I have every sympathy with you."

"Do you think—do you think the poison has spent itself on me? Do you think that if I had children they would suffer?"

"I can only give one answer to that. 'The third and fourth generation,' says the trite old text. You may in time eliminate it from your system, but many years must pass before you can think of marriage."

"I am to be married on Tuesday," whispered the patient.

It was the doctor's turn to be thrilled with horror. There were not many situations which would yield such a sensation to his seasoned nerves. He sat in silence while the babble of the card-table broke in upon them again. "We had a double ruff if you had returned a heart." "I was bound to clear the trumps." They were hot and angry about it.

"How could you?" cried the doctor severely. "It was criminal."

"You forget that I have only learned how I stand to-day." He put his two hands to his temples and pressed them convulsively. "You are a man of the world, Dr. Selby. You have seen or heard of such things before. Give me some advice. I'm in your hands. It is all very sudden and horrible, and I don't think I am strong enough to bear it."

The doctor's heavy brows thickened into two straight lines, and he bit his nails in perplexity.

"The marriage must not take place."

"Then what am I to do?"

"At all costs it must not take place."

"And I must give her up?"

"There can be no question about that."

The young man took out a pocketbook and drew from it a small photograph, holding it out towards the doctor. The firm face softened as he looked at it.

"It is very hard on you, no doubt. I can appreciate it more now that I have seen that. But there is no alternative at all. You must give up all thought of it."

"But this is madness, doctor—madness, I tell you. No, I won't raise my voice. I forgot myself. But realise it, man. I am to be married on Tuesday. This coming Tuesday, you understand. And all the world knows it. How can I put such a public affront upon her. It would be monstrous."

"None the less it must be done. My dear lad, there is no way out of it."

"You would have me simply write brutally and break the engagement at the last moment without a reason. I tell you I couldn't do it."

"I had a patient once who found himself in a somewhat similar situation some years ago," said the doctor thoughtfully. "His device was a singular one. He deliberately committed a penal offence, and so compelled the young lady's people to withdraw their consent to the marriage."

The young baronet shook his head. "My personal honour is as yet unstained," said he. "I have little else left, but that, at least, I will preserve."

"Well, well, it is a nice dilemma, and the choice lies with you."

"Have you no other suggestion?"

"You don't happen to have property in Australia?"

"None."

"But you have capital?"

"Yes."

"Then you could buy some. To-morrow morning would do. A thousand mining shares would be enough. Then you might write to say that urgent business affairs have compelled you to start at an hour's notice to inspect your property. That would give you six months, at any rate."

"Well, that would be possible. Yes, certainly, it would be possible. But think of her position. The house full of wedding presents—guests coming from a distance. It is awful. And you say that there is no alternative."

The doctor shrugged his shoulders.

"Well, then, I might write it now, and start to-morrow—eh? Perhaps you would let me use your desk. Thank you. I am so sorry to keep you from your guests so long. But I won't be a moment now."

He wrote an abrupt note of a few lines. Then with a sudden impulse he tore it to shreds and flung it into the fireplace.

"No, I can't sit down and tell her a lie, doctor," he said rising. "We must find some other way out of this. I will think it over and let you know my decision. You must allow me to double your fee as I have taken such an unconscionable time. Now good-bye, and thank you a thousand times for your sympathy and advice."

"Why, dear me, you haven't even got your prescription yet. This is the mixture, and I should recommend one of these powders every morning, and the chemist will put all directions upon the ointment box. You are placed in a cruel situation, but I trust that these may be but passing clouds. When may I hope to hear from you again?"

"To-morrow morning."

"Very good. How the rain is splashing in the street! You have your waterproof there. You will need it. Good-bye, then, until to-morrow."

He opened the door. A gust of cold, damp air swept into the hall. And yet the doctor stood for a minute or more watching the lonely figure which passed slowly through the yellow splotches of the gas lamps, and into the broad bars of darkness between. It was but his own shadow which trailed up the wall as he passed the lights, and yet it looked to the doctor's eye as though some huge and sombre figure walked by a manikin's side and led him silently up the lonely street.

Dr. Horace Selby heard again of his patient next morning, and rather earlier than he had expected. A paragraph in the Daily News caused him to push away his breakfast untasted, and turned him sick and faint while he read it. "A Deplorable Accident," it was headed, and it ran in this way:

"A fatal accident of a peculiarly painful character is reported from King William Street. About eleven o'clock last night a young man was observed while endeavouring to get out of the way of a hansom to slip and fall under the wheels of a heavy, two-horse dray. On being picked up his injuries were found to be of the most shocking character, and he expired while being conveyed to the hospital. An examination of his pocketbook and cardcase shows beyond any question that the deceased is none other than Sir Francis Norton, of Deane Park, who has only within the last year come into the baronetcy. The accident is made the more deplorable as the deceased, who was only just of age, was on the eve of being married to a young lady belonging to one of the oldest families in the South. With his wealth and his talents the ball of fortune was at his feet, and his many friends will be deeply grieved to know that his promising career has been cut short in so sudden and tragic a fashion."

A FALSE START.

"Is Dr. Horace Wilkinson at home?"

"I am he. Pray step in."

The visitor looked somewhat astonished at having the door opened to him by the master of the house.

"I wanted to have a few words."

The doctor, a pale, nervous young man, dressed in an ultra-professional, long black frock-coat, with a high, white collar cutting off his dapper side-whiskers in the centre, rubbed his hands together and smiled. In the thick, burly man in front of him he scented a patient, and it would be his first. His scanty resources had begun to run somewhat low, and, although he had his first quarter's rent safely locked away in the right-hand drawer of his desk, it was becoming a question with him how he should meet the current expenses of his very simple housekeeping. He bowed, therefore, waved his visitor in, closed the hall door in a careless fashion, as though his own presence thereat had been a purely accidental circumstance, and finally led the burly stranger into his scantily furnished front room, where he motioned him to a seat. Dr. Wilkinson planted himself behind his desk, and, placing his finger-tips together, he gazed with some apprehension at his companion. What was the matter with the man? He seemed very red in the face. Some of his old professors would have diagnosed his case by now, and would have electrified the patient by describing his own symptoms before he had said a word about them. Dr. Horace Wilkinson racked his brains for some clue, but Nature had fashioned him as a plodder—a very reliable plodder and nothing more. He could think of nothing save that the visitor's watch-chain had a very brassy appearance, with a corollary to the effect that he would be lucky if he got half-a-crown out of him. Still, even half-a-crown was something in those early days of struggle.

Whilst the doctor had been running his eyes over the stranger, the latter had been plunging his hands into pocket after pocket of his heavy coat. The heat of the weather, his dress, and this exercise of pocket-rummaging had all combined to still further redden his face, which had changed from brick to beet, with a gloss of moisture on his brow. This extreme ruddiness brought a clue at last to the observant doctor. Surely it was not to be attained without alcohol. In alcohol lay the secret of this man's trouble. Some little delicacy was needed, however, in showing him that he had read his case aright—that at a glance he had penetrated to the inmost sources of his ailments.

"It's very hot," observed the stranger, mopping his forehead.

"Yes, it is weather which tempts one to drink rather more beer than is good for one," answered Dr. Horace Wilkinson, looking very knowingly at his companion from over his finger-tips.

"Dear, dear, you shouldn't do that."

"I! I never touch beer."

"Neither do I. I've been an abstainer for twenty years."

This was depressing. Dr. Wilkinson blushed until he was nearly as red as the other. "May I ask what I can do for you?" he asked, picking up his stethoscope and tapping it gently against his thumb-nail.

"Yes, I was just going to tell you. I heard of your coming, but I couldn't get round before——" He broke into a nervous little cough.

"Yes?" said the doctor encouragingly.

"I should have been here three weeks ago, but you know how these things get put off." He coughed again behind his large red hand.

"I do not think that you need say anything more," said the doctor, taking over the case with an easy air of command. "Your cough is quite sufficient. It is entirely bronchial by the sound. No doubt the mischief is circumscribed at present, but there is always the danger that it may spread, so you have done wisely to come to me. A little judicious treatment will soon set you right. Your waistcoat, please, but not your shirt. Puff out your chest and say ninety-nine in a deep voice."

The red-faced man began to laugh. "It's all right, doctor," said he. "That cough comes from chewing tobacco, and I know it's a very bad habit. Nine-and-ninepence is what I have to say to you, for I'm the officer of the gas company, and they have a claim against you for that on the metre."

Dr. Horace Wilkinson collapsed into his chair. "Then you're not a patient?" he gasped.

"Never needed a doctor in my life, sir."

"Oh, that's all right." The doctor concealed his disappointment under an affectation of facetiousness. "You don't look as if you troubled them much. I don't know what we should do if every one were as robust. I shall call at the company's offices and pay this small amount."

"If you could make it convenient, sir, now that I am here, it would save trouble ____"

"Oh, certainly!" These eternal little sordid money troubles were more trying to the doctor than plain living or scanty food. He took out his purse and slid the contents on to the table. There were two half-crowns and some pennies. In his drawer he had ten golden sovereigns. But those were his rent. If he once broke in upon them he was lost. He would starve first.

"Dear me!" said he, with a smile, as at some strange, unheard-of incident. "I have run short of small change. I am afraid I shall have to call upon the company, after all."

"Very well, sir." The inspector rose, and with a practised glance around, which valued every article in the room, from the two-guinea carpet to the eight-shilling muslin curtains, he took his departure.

When he had gone Dr. Wilkinson rearranged his room, as was his habit a dozen times in the day. He laid out his large Quain's Dictionary of Medicine in the forefront of the table so as to impress the casual patient that he had ever the best authorities at his elbow. Then he cleared all the little instruments out of his pocket-case—the scissors, the forceps, the bistouries, the lancets—and he laid them all out beside the stethoscope, to make as good a show as possible. His ledger, day-book, and visiting-book were spread in front of him. There was no entry in any of them yet, but it would not look well to have the covers too glossy and new, so he rubbed them together and daubed ink over them. Neither would it be well that any patient should observe that his name was the first in the book, so he filled up the first page of each with notes of imaginary visits paid to nameless patients during the last three weeks. Having done all this, he rested his head upon his hands and relapsed into the terrible occupation of waiting.

Terrible enough at any time to the young professional man, but most of all to one who knows that the weeks, and even the days during which he can hold out are numbered. Economise as he would, the money would still slip away in the countless little claims which a man never understands until he lives under a rooftree of his own. Dr. Wilkinson could not deny, as he sat at his desk and looked at the little heap of silver and coppers, that his chances of being a successful practitioner in Sutton were rapidly vanishing away.

And yet it was a bustling, prosperous town, with so much money in it that it seemed strange that a man with a trained brain and dexterous fingers should be starved out of it for want of employment. At his desk, Dr. Horace Wilkinson could see the never-ending double current of people which ebbed and flowed in front of his window. It was a busy street, and the air was forever filled with the dull roar of life, the grinding of the wheels, and the patter of countless feet. Men, women, and children, thousands and thousands of them passed in the day, and yet each was hurrying on upon his own business, scarce glancing at the small brass plate, or wasting a thought upon the man who waited in the front room. And yet how many of them would obviously, glaringly have been the better for his professional assistance. Dyspeptic men, anemic women, blotched faces, bilious complexions—they flowed past him, they needing him, he needing them, and yet the remorseless bar of professional etiquette kept them forever apart. What could he do? Could he stand at his own front door, pluck the casual stranger by the sleeve, and whisper in his ear, "Sir, you will forgive me for remarking that you are suffering from a severe attack of acne rosacea, which makes you a peculiarly unpleasant object. Allow me to suggest that a small prescription containing arsenic, which will not cost you more than you often spend upon a single meal, will be very much to your advantage." Such an address would be a degradation to the high and lofty profession of Medicine, and there are no such sticklers for the ethics of that profession as some to whom she has been but a bitter and a grudging mother.

Dr. Horace Wilkinson was still looking moodily out of the window, when there came a sharp clang at the bell. Often it had rung, and with every ring his hopes had sprung up, only to dwindle away again, and change to leaden disappointment, as he faced some beggar or touting tradesman. But the doctor's spirit was young and elastic, and again, in spite of all experience, it responded to that exhilarating summons. He sprang to his feet, cast his eyes over the table, thrust out his medical books a little more prominently, and hurried to the door. A groan escaped him as he entered the hall. He could see through the half-glazed upper panels that a gypsy van, hung round with wicker tables and chairs, had halted before his door, and that a couple of the vagrants, with a baby, were waiting outside. He had learned by experience that it was better not even to parley with such people.

"I have nothing for you," said he, loosing the latch by an inch. "Go away!"

He closed the door, but the bell clanged once more. "Get away! Get away!" he cried impatiently, and walked back into his consulting-room. He had hardly seated himself when the bell went for the third time. In a towering passion he rushed back, flung open the door.

"What the——?"

"If you please, sir, we need a doctor."

In an instant he was rubbing his hands again with his blandest professional smile. These were patients, then, whom he had tried to hunt from his doorstep —the very first patients, whom he had waited for so impatiently. They did not look very promising. The man, a tall, lank-haired gypsy, had gone back to the horse's head. There remained a small, hard-faced woman with a great bruise all round her eye. She wore a yellow silk handkerchief round her head, and a baby, tucked in a red shawl, was pressed to her bosom.

"Pray step in, madam," said Dr. Horace Wilkinson, with his very best sympathetic manner. In this case, at least, there could be no mistake as to diagnosis. "If you will sit on this sofa, I shall very soon make you feel much more comfortable."

He poured a little water from his carafe into a saucer, made a compress of lint, fastened it over the injured eye, and secured the whole with a spica bandage, secundum artem.

"Thank ye kindly, sir," said the woman, when his work was finished; "that's nice and warm, and may God bless your honour. But it wasn't about my eye at all that I came to see a doctor."

"Not your eye?" Dr. Horace Wilkinson was beginning to be a little doubtful as to the advantages of quick diagnosis. It is an excellent thing to be able to surprise a patient, but hitherto it was always the patient who had surprised him.

"The baby's got the measles."

The mother parted the red shawl, and exhibited a little dark, black-eyed gypsy baby, whose swarthy face was all flushed and mottled with a dark-red rash. The child breathed with a rattling sound, and it looked up at the doctor with eyes which were heavy with want of sleep and crusted together at the lids.

"Hum! Yes. Measles, sure enough—and a smart attack."

"I just wanted you to see her, sir, so that you could signify."

"Could what?"

"Signify, if anything happened."

"Oh, I see—certify."

"And now that you've seen it, sir, I'll go on, for Reuben—that's my man—is in a hurry."

"But don't you want any medicine?"

"Oh, now you've seen it, it's all right. I'll let you know if anything happens."

"But you must have some medicine. The child is very ill." He descended into the little room which he had fitted as a surgery, and he made up a two-ounce bottle of cooling medicine. In such cities as Sutton there are few patients who can afford to pay a fee to both doctor and chemist, so that unless the physician is prepared to play the part of both he will have little chance of making a living at either.

"There is your medicine, madam. You will find the directions upon the bottle. Keep the child warm and give it a light diet."

"Thank you kindly, sir." She shouldered her baby and marched for the door.

"Excuse me, madam," said the doctor nervously. "Don't you think it too small a matter to make a bill of? Perhaps it would be better if we had a settlement at once."

The gypsy woman looked at him reproachfully out of her one uncovered eye.

"Are you going to charge me for that?" she asked. "How much, then?"

"Well, say half-a-crown." He mentioned the sum in a half-jesting way, as though it were too small to take serious notice of, but the gypsy woman raised quite a scream at the mention of it.

"'Arf-a-crown! for that?"

"Well, my good woman, why not go to the poor doctor if you cannot afford a fee?"

She fumbled in her pocket, craning awkwardly to keep her grip upon the baby.

"Here's sevenpence," she said at last, holding out a little pile of copper coins. "I'll give you that and a wicker footstool."

"But my fee is half-a-crown." The doctor's views of the glory of his profession cried out against this wretched haggling, and yet what was he to do? "Where am I to get 'arf-a-crown? It is well for gentlefolk like you who sit in your grand houses, and can eat and drink what you like, an' charge 'arf-a-crown for just saying as much as, "Ow d'ye do?' We can't pick up' arf-crowns like that. What we gets we earns 'ard. This sevenpence is just all I've got. You told me to feed the child light. She must feed light, for what she's to have is more than I know."

Whilst the woman had been speaking, Dr. Horace Wilkinson's eyes had wandered to the tiny heap of money upon the table, which represented all that separated him from absolute starvation, and he chuckled to himself at the grim joke that he should appear to this poor woman to be a being living in the lap of luxury. Then he picked up the odd coppers, leaving only the two half-crowns upon the table.

"Here you are," he said brusquely. "Never mind the fee, and take these coppers. They may be of some use to you. Good-bye!" He bowed her out, and closed the door behind her. After all she was the thin edge of the wedge. These wandering people have great powers of recommendation. All large practices have been built up from such foundations. The hangers-on to the kitchen recommend to the kitchen, they to the drawing-room, and so it spreads. At least he could say now that he had had a patient.

He went into the back room and lit the spirit-kettle to boil the water for his tea, laughing the while at the recollection of his recent interview. If all patients were like this one it could easily be reckoned how many it would take to ruin him completely. Putting aside the dirt upon his carpet and the loss of time, there were twopence gone upon the bandage, fourpence or more upon the medicine, to say nothing of phial, cork, label, and paper. Then he had given her fivepence, so that his first patient had absorbed altogether not less than one sixth of his available capital. If five more were to come he would be a broken man. He sat down upon the portmanteau and shook with laughter at the thought, while he measured out his one spoonful and a half of tea at one shilling eightpence into the brown earthenware teapot. Suddenly, however, the laugh faded from his face, and he cocked his ear towards the door, standing listening with a slanting head and a sidelong eye. There had been a rasping of wheels against the curb, the sound of steps outside, and then a loud peal at the bell. With his teaspoon in his hand he peeped round the corner and saw with amazement that a carriage and pair were waiting outside, and that a powdered footman was standing at the door. The spoon tinkled down upon the floor, and he stood gazing in bewilderment. Then, pulling himself together, he threw open the door.

"Young man," said the flunky, "tell your master, Dr. Wilkinson, that he is wanted just as quick as ever he can come to Lady Millbank, at the Towers. He is to come this very instant. We'd take him with us, but we have to go back to see if Dr. Mason is home yet. Just you stir your stumps and give him the message."

The footman nodded and was off in an instant, while the coachman lashed his horses and the carriage flew down the street.

Here was a new development. Dr. Horace Wilkinson stood at his door and tried to think it all out. Lady Millbank, of the Towers! People of wealth and position, no doubt. And a serious case, or why this haste and summoning of two doctors? But, then, why in the name of all that is wonderful should he be sent for?

He was obscure, unknown, without influence. There must be some mistake. Yes, that must be the true explanation; or was it possible that some one was attempting a cruel hoax upon him? At any rate, it was too positive a message to be disregarded. He must set off at once and settle the matter one way or the other.

But he had one source of information. At the corner of the street was a small shop where one of the oldest inhabitants dispensed newspapers and gossip. He could get information there if anywhere. He put on his well-brushed top hat, secreted instruments and bandages in all his pockets, and without waiting for his tea closed up his establishment and started off upon his adventure.

The stationer at the corner was a human directory to every one and everything in Sutton, so that he soon had all the information which he wanted. Sir John Millbank was very well known in the town, it seemed. He was a merchant prince, an exporter of pens, three times mayor, and reported to be fully worth two millions sterling.

The Towers was his palatial seat, just outside the city. His wife had been an invalid for some years, and was growing worse. So far the whole thing seemed to be genuine enough. By some amazing chance these people really had sent for him.

And then another doubt assailed him, and he turned back into the shop.

"I am your neighbour, Dr. Horace Wilkinson," said he. "Is there any other medical man of that name in the town?"

No, the stationer was quite positive that there was not.

That was final, then. A great good fortune had come in his way, and he must take prompt advantage of it. He called a cab and drove furiously to the Towers, with his brain in a whirl, giddy with hope and delight at one moment, and sickened with fears and doubts at the next lest the case should in some way be beyond his powers, or lest he should find at some critical moment that he was without the instrument or appliance that was needed. Every strange and outre case of which he had ever heard or read came back into his mind, and long before he reached the Towers he had worked himself into a positive conviction that he would be instantly required to do a trephining at the least.

The Towers was a very large house, standing back amid trees, at the head of a winding drive. As he drove up the doctor sprang out, paid away half his worldly assets as a fare, and followed a stately footman who, having taken his name, led him through the oak-panelled, stained-glass hall, gorgeous with deers' heads and ancient armour, and ushered him into a large sitting-room beyond. A very irritable-looking, acid-faced man was seated in an armchair by the fireplace, while two young ladies in white were standing together in the bow window at the further end.

"Hullo! hullo! hullo! What's this—heh?" cried the irritable man. "Are you Dr. Wilkinson? Eh?"

"Yes, sir, I am Dr. Wilkinson."

"Really, now. You seem very young—much younger than I expected. Well, well, well, Mason's old, and yet he don't seem to know much about it. I suppose we must try the other end now. You're the Wilkinson who wrote something about the lungs? Heh?"

Here was a light! The only two letters which the doctor had ever written to The Lancet—modest little letters thrust away in a back column among the wrangles about medical ethics and the inquiries as to how much it took to keep a horse in the country—had been upon pulmonary disease. They had not been wasted, then. Some eye had picked them out and marked the name of the writer. Who could say that work was ever wasted, or that merit did not promptly meet with its reward?

"Yes, I have written on the subject."

"Ha! Well, then, where's Mason?"

"I have not the pleasure of his acquaintance."

"No?—that's queer too. He knows you and thinks a lot of your opinion. You're a stranger in the town, are you not?"

"Yes, I have only been here a very short time."

"That was what Mason said. He didn't give me the address. Said he would call on you and bring you, but when the wife got worse of course I inquired for you and sent for you direct. I sent for Mason, too, but he was out. However, we can't wait for him, so just run away upstairs and do what you can."

"Well, I am placed in a rather delicate position," said Dr. Horace Wilkinson, with some hesitation. "I am here, as I understand, to meet my colleague, Dr. Mason, in consultation. It would, perhaps, hardly be correct for me to see the patient in his absence. I think that I would rather wait."

"Would you, by Jove! Do you think I'll let my wife get worse while the doctor is coolly kicking his heels in the room below? No, sir, I am a plain man, and I tell you that you will either go up or go out."

The style of speech jarred upon the doctor's sense of the fitness of things, but still when a man's wife is ill much may be overlooked. He contented himself by bowing somewhat stiffly. "I shall go up, if you insist upon it," said he.

"I do insist upon it. And another thing, I won't have her thumped about all over the chest, or any hocus-pocus of the sort. She has bronchitis and asthma, and that's all. If you can cure it well and good. But it only weakens her to have you tapping and listening, and it does no good either."

Personal disrespect was a thing that the doctor could stand; but the profession was to him a holy thing, and a flippant word about it cut him to the quick.

"Thank you," said he, picking up his hat. "I have the honour to wish you a very good day. I do not care to undertake the responsibility of this case."

"Hullo! what's the matter now?"

"It is not my habit to give opinions without examining my patient. I wonder that you should suggest such a course to a medical man. I wish you good day."

But Sir John Millbank was a commercial man, and believed in the commercial principle that the more difficult a thing is to attain the more valuable it is. A doctor's opinion had been to him a mere matter of guineas. But here was a young man who seemed to care nothing either for his wealth or title. His respect for his judgment increased amazingly.

"Tut! tut!" said he; "Mason is not so thin-skinned. There! there! Have your way! Do what you like and I won't say another word. I'll just run upstairs and tell Lady Millbank that you are coming."

The door had hardly closed behind him when the two demure young ladies darted out of their corner, and fluttered with joy in front of the astonished doctor.

"Oh, well done! well done!" cried the taller, clapping her hands.

"Don't let him bully you, doctor," said the other. "Oh, it was so nice to hear you stand up to him. That's the way he does with poor Dr. Mason. Dr. Mason has never examined mamma yet. He always takes papa's word for everything. Hush, Maude; here he comes again." They subsided in an instant into their corner as silent and demure as ever.

Dr. Horace Wilkinson followed Sir John up the broad, thick-carpeted staircase, and into the darkened sick room. In a quarter of an hour he had sounded and sifted the case to the uttermost, and descended with the husband once more to the drawing-room. In front of the fireplace were standing two gentlemen, the one a very typical, clean-shaven, general practitioner, the other a striking-looking man of middle age, with pale blue eyes and a long red beard.

"Hullo, Mason, you've come at last!"

"Yes, Sir John, and I have brought, as I promised, Dr. Wilkinson with me."

"Dr. Wilkinson! Why, this is he."

Dr. Mason stared in astonishment. "I have never seen the gentleman before!" he cried.

"Nevertheless I am Dr. Wilkinson—Dr. Horace Wilkinson, of 114 Canal View."

"Good gracious, Sir John!" cried Dr. Mason.

"Did you think that in a case of such importance I should call in a junior local practitioner! This is Dr. Adam Wilkinson, lecturer on pulmonary diseases at Regent's College, London, physician upon the staff of the St. Swithin's Hospital, and author of a dozen works upon the subject. He happened to be in Sutton upon a visit, and I thought I would utilise his presence to have a first-rate opinion upon Lady Millbank."

"Thank you," said Sir John, dryly. "But I fear my wife is rather tired now, for she has just been very thoroughly examined by this young gentleman. I think we will let it stop at that for the present; though, of course, as you have had the trouble of coming here, I should be glad to have a note of your fees."

When Dr. Mason had departed, looking very disgusted, and his friend, the specialist, very amused, Sir John listened to all the young physician had to say about the case.

"Now, I'll tell you what," said he, when he had finished. "I'm a man of my word, d'ye see? When I like a man I freeze to him. I'm a good friend and a bad enemy. I believe in you, and I don't believe in Mason. From now on you are my doctor, and that of my family. Come and see my wife every day. How does that suit your book?"

"I am extremely grateful to you for your kind intentions toward me, but I am afraid there is no possible way in which I can avail myself of them."

"Heh! what d'ye mean?"

"I could not possibly take Dr. Mason's place in the middle of a case like this. It would be a most unprofessional act."

"Oh, well, go your own way!" cried Sir John, in despair. "Never was such a man for making difficulties. You've had a fair offer and you've refused it, and now you can just go your own way."

The millionaire stumped out of the room in a huff, and Dr. Horace Wilkinson made his way homeward to his spirit-lamp and his one-and-eightpenny tea, with his first guinea in his pocket, and with a feeling that he had upheld the best traditions of his profession.

And yet this false start of his was a true start also, for it soon came to Dr.

Mason's ears that his junior had had it in his power to carry off his best patient and had forborne to do so. To the honour of the profession be it said that such forbearance is the rule rather than the exception, and yet in this case, with so very junior a practitioner and so very wealthy a patient, the temptation was greater than is usual. There was a grateful note, a visit, a friendship, and now the well-known firm of Mason and Wilkinson is doing the largest family practice in Sutton.

THE CURSE OF EVE.

Robert Johnson was an essentially commonplace man, with no feature to distinguish him from a million others. He was pale of face, ordinary in looks, neutral in opinions, thirty years of age, and a married man. By trade he was a gentleman's outfitter in the New North Road, and the competition of business squeezed out of him the little character that was left. In his hope of conciliating customers he had become cringing and pliable, until working ever in the same routine from day to day he seemed to have sunk into a soulless machine rather than a man. No great question had ever stirred him. At the end of this snug century, self-contained in his own narrow circle, it seemed impossible that any of the mighty, primitive passions of mankind could ever reach him. Yet birth, and lust, and illness, and death are changeless things, and when one of these harsh facts springs out upon a man at some sudden turn of the path of life, it dashes off for the moment his mask of civilisation and gives a glimpse of the stranger and stronger face below.

Johnson's wife was a quiet little woman, with brown hair and gentle ways. His affection for her was the one positive trait in his character. Together they would lay out the shop window every Monday morning, the spotless shirts in their green cardboard boxes below, the neckties above hung in rows over the brass rails, the cheap studs glistening from the white cards at either side, while in the background were the rows of cloth caps and the bank of boxes in which the more valuable hats were screened from the sunlight. She kept the books and sent out the bills. No one but she knew the joys and sorrows which crept into his small life. She had shared his exultations when the gentleman who was going to India had bought ten dozen shirts and an incredible number of collars, and she had been as stricken as he when, after the goods had gone, the bill was returned from the hotel address with the intimation that no such person had lodged there. For five years they had worked, building up the business, thrown together all the more closely because their marriage had been a childless one. Now, however, there were signs that a change was at hand, and that speedily. She was unable to come downstairs, and her mother, Mrs. Peyton, came over from Camberwell to nurse her and to welcome her grandchild.

Little qualms of anxiety came over Johnson as his wife's time approached. However, after all, it was a natural process. Other men's wives went through it unharmed, and why should not his? He was himself one of a family of fourteen, and yet his mother was alive and hearty. It was quite the exception for anything to go wrong. And yet in spite of his reasonings the remembrance of his wife's condition was always like a sombre background to all his other thoughts.

Dr. Miles of Bridport Place, the best man in the neighbourhood, was retained five months in advance, and, as time stole on, many little packets of absurdly small white garments with frill work and ribbons began to arrive among the big consignments of male necessities. And then one evening, as Johnson was ticketing the scarfs in the shop, he heard a bustle upstairs, and Mrs. Peyton came running down to say that Lucy was bad and that she thought the doctor ought to be there without delay.

It was not Robert Johnson's nature to hurry. He was prim and staid and liked to do things in an orderly fashion. It was a quarter of a mile from the corner of the New North Road where his shop stood to the doctor's house in Bridport Place. There were no cabs in sight so he set off upon foot, leaving the lad to mind the shop. At Bridport Place he was told that the doctor had just gone to Harman Street to attend a man in a fit. Johnson started off for Harman Street, losing a little of his primness as he became more anxious. Two full cabs but no empty ones passed him on the way. At Harman Street he learned that the doctor had gone on to a case of measles, fortunately he had left the address— 69 Dunstan Road, at the other side of the Regent's Canal. Robert's primness had vanished now as he thought of the women waiting at home, and he began to run as hard as he could down the Kingsland Road. Some way along he sprang into a cab which stood by the curb and drove to Dunstan Road. The doctor had just left, and Robert Johnson felt inclined to sit down upon the steps in despair.

Fortunately he had not sent the cab away, and he was soon back at Bridport Place. Dr. Miles had not returned yet, but they were expecting him every instant. Johnson waited, drumming his fingers on his knees, in a high, dim lit room, the air of which was charged with a faint, sickly smell of ether. The furniture was massive, and the books in the shelves were sombre, and a squat black clock ticked mournfully on the mantelpiece. It told him that it was half-past seven, and that he had been gone an hour and a quarter. Whatever would the women think of him! Every time that a distant door slammed he sprang from his chair in a quiver of eagerness. His ears strained to catch the deep notes of the doctor's voice. And then, suddenly, with a gush of joy he heard a quick step outside, and the sharp click of the key in the lock. In an instant he was out in the hall, before the doctor's foot was over the threshold.

"If you please, doctor, I've come for you," he cried; "the wife was taken bad at six o'clock."

He hardly knew what he expected the doctor to do. Something very energetic, certainly—to seize some drugs, perhaps, and rush excitedly with him through the gaslit streets. Instead of that Dr. Miles threw his umbrella into the rack, jerked off his hat with a somewhat peevish gesture, and pushed Johnson back into the room.

"Let's see! You DID engage me, didn't you?" he asked in no very cordial voice.

"Oh, yes, doctor, last November. Johnson the outfitter, you know, in the New North Road."

"Yes, yes. It's a bit overdue," said the doctor, glancing at a list of names in a note-book with a very shiny cover. "Well, how is she?"

"I don't——"

"Ah, of course, it's your first. You'll know more about it next time."

"Mrs. Peyton said it was time you were there, sir."

"My dear sir, there can be no very pressing hurry in a first case. We shall have an all-night affair, I fancy. You can't get an engine to go without coals, Mr. Johnson, and I have had nothing but a light lunch."

"We could have something cooked for you—something hot and a cup of tea."

"Thank you, but I fancy my dinner is actually on the table. I can do no good in the earlier stages. Go home and say that I am coming, and I will be round immediately afterwards."

A sort of horror filled Robert Johnson as he gazed at this man who could think about his dinner at such a moment. He had not imagination enough to realise that the experience which seemed so appallingly important to him, was the merest everyday matter of business to the medical man who could not have lived for a year had he not, amid the rush of work, remembered what was due to his own health. To Johnson he seemed little better than a monster. His thoughts were bitter as he sped back to his shop.

"You've taken your time," said his mother-in-law reproachfully, looking down the stairs as he entered.

"I couldn't help it!" he gasped. "Is it over?"

"Over! She's got to be worse, poor dear, before she can be better. Where's Dr. Miles!"

"He's coming after he's had dinner." The old woman was about to make some reply, when, from the half-opened door behind a high whinnying voice cried out for her. She ran back and closed the door, while Johnson, sick at heart, turned into the shop. There he sent the lad home and busied himself frantically in putting up shutters and turning out boxes. When all was closed and finished he seated himself in the parlour behind the shop. But he could not sit still. He rose incessantly to walk a few paces and then fell back into a chair once more. Suddenly the clatter of china fell upon his ear, and he saw the maid pass the door with a cup on a tray and a smoking teapot.

"Who is that for, Jane?" he asked.

"For the mistress, Mr. Johnson. She says she would fancy it."

There was immeasurable consolation to him in that homely cup of tea. It wasn't so very bad after all if his wife could think of such things. So light-hearted was he that he asked for a cup also. He had just finished it when the doctor arrived, with a small black leather bag in his hand.

"Well, how is she?" he asked genially.

"Oh, she's very much better," said Johnson, with enthusiasm.

"Dear me, that's bad!" said the doctor. "Perhaps it will do if I look in on my morning round?"

"No, no," cried Johnson, clutching at his thick frieze overcoat. "We are so glad that you have come. And, doctor, please come down soon and let me know what you think about it."

The doctor passed upstairs, his firm, heavy steps resounding through the house. Johnson could hear his boots creaking as he walked about the floor above him, and the sound was a consolation to him. It was crisp and decided, the tread of a man who had plenty of self-confidence. Presently, still straining his ears to catch what was going on, he heard the scraping of a chair as it was drawn along the floor, and a moment later he heard the door fly open and someone come rushing downstairs. Johnson sprang up with his hair bristling, thinking that some dreadful thing had occurred, but it was only his mother-in-law, incoherent with excitement and searching for scissors and some tape. She vanished again and Jane passed up the stairs with a pile of newly aired linen. Then, after an interval of silence, Johnson heard the heavy, creaking tread and the doctor came down into the parlour.

"That's better," said he, pausing with his hand upon the door. "You look pale, Mr. Johnson."

"Oh no, sir, not at all," he answered deprecatingly, mopping his brow with his handkerchief.

"There is no immediate cause for alarm," said Dr. Miles. "The case is not all that we could wish it. Still we will hope for the best."

"Is there danger, sir?" gasped Johnson.

"Well, there is always danger, of course. It is not altogether a favourable case, but still it might be much worse. I have given her a draught. I saw as I passed that they have been doing a little building opposite to you. It's an improving quarter. The rents go higher and higher. You have a lease of your own little place, eh?"

"Yes, sir, yes!" cried Johnson, whose ears were straining for every sound from above, and who felt none the less that it was very soothing that the doctor should be able to chat so easily at such a time. "That's to say no, sir, I am a yearly tenant."

"Ah, I should get a lease if I were you. There's Marshall, the watchmaker, down the street. I attended his wife twice and saw him through the typhoid when they took up the drains in Prince Street. I assure you his landlord sprung his rent nearly forty a year and he had to pay or clear out."

"Did his wife get through it, doctor?"

"Oh yes, she did very well. Hullo! hullo!"

He slanted his ear to the ceiling with a questioning face, and then darted swiftly from the room.

It was March and the evenings were chill, so Jane had lit the fire, but the wind drove the smoke downwards and the air was full of its acrid taint. Johnson felt chilled to the bone, though rather by his apprehensions than by the weather. He crouched over the fire with his thin white hands held out to the blaze. At ten o'clock Jane brought in the joint of cold meat and laid his place for supper, but he could not bring himself to touch it. He drank a glass of the beer, however, and felt the better for it. The tension of his nerves seemed to have reacted upon his hearing, and he was able to follow the most trivial things in the room above. Once, when the beer was still heartening him, he nerved himself to creep on tiptoe up the stair and to listen to what was going on. The bedroom door was half an inch open, and through the slit he could catch a glimpse of the clean-shaven face of the doctor, looking wearier and more anxious than before. Then he rushed downstairs like a lunatic, and running to the door he tried to distract his thoughts by watching what; was going on in the street. The shops were all shut, and some rollicking boon companions came shouting along from the public-house. He stayed at the door until the stragglers had thinned down, and then came back to his seat by the fire. In his dim brain he was asking himself questions which had never intruded themselves before. Where was the justice of it? What had his sweet, innocent little wife done that she should be used so? Why was nature so cruel? He was frightened at his own thoughts, and yet wondered that they had never occurred to him before.

As the early morning drew in, Johnson, sick at heart and shivering in every limb, sat with his great coat huddled round him, staring at the grey ashes and waiting hopelessly for some relief. His face was white and clammy, and his nerves had been numbed into a half conscious state by the long monotony of misery. But suddenly all his feelings leapt into keen life again as he heard the bedroom door open and the doctor's steps upon the stair. Robert Johnson was precise and unemotional in everyday life, but he almost shrieked now as he rushed forward to know if it were over.

One glance at the stern, drawn face which met him showed that it was no pleasant news which had sent the doctor downstairs. His appearance had altered as much as Johnson's during the last few hours. His hair was on end, his face flushed, his forehead dotted with beads of perspiration. There was a peculiar fierceness in his eye, and about the lines of his mouth, a fighting look as befitted a man who for hours on end had been striving with the hungriest of foes for the most precious of prizes. But there was a sadness too, as though his grim opponent had been overmastering him. He sat down and leaned his head upon his hand like a man who is fagged out.

"I thought it my duty to see you, Mr. Johnson, and to tell you that it is a very nasty case. Your wife's heart is not strong, and she has some symptoms which I do not like. What I wanted to say is that if you would like to have a second opinion I shall be very glad to meet anyone whom you might suggest."

Johnson was so dazed by his want of sleep and the evil news that he could hardly grasp the doctor's meaning. The other, seeing him hesitate, thought that he was considering the expense.

"Smith or Hawley would come for two guineas," said he. "But I think Pritchard of the City Road is the best man."

"Oh, yes, bring the best man," cried Johnson.

"Pritchard would want three guineas. He is a senior man, you see."

"I'd give him all I have if he would pull her through. Shall I run for him?"

"Yes. Go to my house first and ask for the green baize bag. The assistant will give it to you. Tell him I want the A. C. E. mixture. Her heart is too weak for chloroform. Then go for Pritchard and bring him back with you."

It was heavenly for Johnson to have something to do and to feel that he was of some use to his wife. He ran swiftly to Bridport Place, his footfalls clattering through the silent streets and the big dark policemen turning their yellow funnels of light on him as he passed. Two tugs at the night-bell brought down a sleepy, half-clad assistant, who handed him a stoppered glass bottle and a cloth bag which contained something which clinked when you moved it. Johnson thrust the bottle into his pocket, seized the green bag, and pressing his hat firmly down ran as hard as he could set foot to ground until he was in the City Road and saw the name of Pritchard engraved in white upon a red ground. He bounded in triumph up the three steps which led to the door, and as he did so there was a crash behind him. His precious bottle was in fragments upon the pavement.

For a moment he felt as if it were his wife's body that was lying there. But the run had freshened his wits and he saw that the mischief might be repaired. He pulled vigorously at the night-bell.

"Well, what's the matter?" asked a gruff voice at his elbow. He started back and looked up at the windows, but there was no sign of life. He was approaching the bell again with the intention of pulling it, when a perfect roar burst from the wall.

"I can't stand shivering here all night," cried the voice. "Say who you are and what you want or I shut the tube."

Then for the first time Johnson saw that the end of a speaking-tube hung out of the wall just above the bell. He shouted up it,—

"I want you to come with me to meet Dr. Miles at a confinement at once."

"How far?" shrieked the irascible voice.

"The New North Road, Hoxton."

"My consultation fee is three guineas, payable at the time."

"All right," shouted Johnson. "You are to bring a bottle of A. C. E. mixture with you."

"All right! Wait a bit!"

Five minutes later an elderly, hard-faced man, with grizzled hair, flung open the door. As he emerged a voice from somewhere in the shadows cried,—

"Mind you take your cravat, John," and he impatiently growled something over his shoulder in reply.

The consultant was a man who had been hardened by a life of ceaseless labour, and who had been driven, as so many others have been, by the needs of his own increasing family to set the commercial before the philanthropic side of his profession. Yet beneath his rough crust he was a man with a kindly heart.

"We don't want to break a record," said he, pulling up and panting after attempting to keep up with Johnson for five minutes. "I would go quicker if I could, my dear sir, and I quite sympathise with your anxiety, but really I can't manage it."

So Johnson, on fire with impatience, had to slow down until they reached the New North Road, when he ran ahead and had the door open for the doctor when he came. He heard the two meet outside the bed-room, and caught scraps of their conversation. "Sorry to knock you up—nasty case—decent people." Then it sank into a mumble and the door closed behind them.

Johnson sat up in his chair now, listening keenly, for he knew that a crisis must be at hand. He heard the two doctors moving about, and was able to distinguish the step of Pritchard, which had a drag in it, from the clean, crisp sound of the other's footfall. There was silence for a few minutes and then a curious drunken, mumbling sing-song voice came quavering up, very unlike anything which he had heard hitherto. At the same time a sweetish, insidious scent, imperceptible perhaps to any nerves less strained than his, crept down the stairs and penetrated into the room. The voice dwindled into a mere drone and finally sank away into silence, and Johnson gave a long sigh of relief, for he knew that the drug had done its work and that, come what might, there should be no more pain for the sufferer.

But soon the silence became even more trying to him than the cries had been. He had no clue now as to what was going on, and his mind swarmed with horrible possibilities. He rose and went to the bottom of the stairs again. He heard the clink of metal against metal, and the subdued murmur of the doctors' voices. Then he heard Mrs. Peyton say something, in a tone as of fear or expostulation, and again the doctors murmured together. For twenty minutes he stood there leaning against the wall, listening to the occasional rumbles of talk without being able to catch a word of it. And then of a sudden there rose out of the silence the strangest little piping cry, and Mrs. Peyton screamed out in her delight and the man ran into the parlour and flung himself down upon the horse-hair sofa, drumming his heels on it in his ecstasy.

But often the great cat Fate lets us go only to clutch us again in a fiercer grip. As minute after minute passed and still no sound came from above save those thin, glutinous cries, Johnson cooled from his frenzy of joy, and lay breathless with his ears straining. They were moving slowly about. They were talking in subdued tones. Still minute after minute passing, and no word from the voice for which he listened. His nerves were dulled by his night of trouble, and he waited in limp wretchedness upon his sofa. There he still sat when the doctors came down to him—a bedraggled, miserable figure with his face grimy and his hair unkempt from his long vigil. He rose as they entered, bracing himself against the mantelpiece.

"Is she dead?" he asked.

"Doing well," answered the doctor.

And at the words that little conventional spirit which had never known until that night the capacity for fierce agony which lay within it, learned for the second time that there were springs of joy also which it had never tapped before. His impulse was to fall upon his knees, but he was shy before the doctors.

"Can I go up?"

"In a few minutes."

"I'm sure, doctor, I'm very—I'm very——" he grew inarticulate. "Here are your three guineas, Dr. Pritchard. I wish they were three hundred."

"So do I," said the senior man, and they laughed as they shook hands.

Johnson opened the shop door for them and heard their talk as they stood for an instant outside.

"Looked nasty at one time."

"Very glad to have your help."

"Delighted, I'm sure. Won't you step round and have a cup of coffee?"

"No, thanks. I'm expecting another case."

The firm step and the dragging one passed away to the right and the left. Johnson turned from the door still with that turmoil of joy in his heart. He seemed to be making a new start in life. He felt that he was a stronger and a deeper man. Perhaps all this suffering had an object then. It might prove to be a blessing both to his wife and to him. The very thought was one which he would have been incapable of conceiving twelve hours before. He was full of new emotions. If there had been a harrowing there had been a planting too.

"Can I come up?" he cried, and then, without waiting for an answer, he took the steps three at a time.

Mrs. Peyton was standing by a soapy bath with a bundle in her hands. From under the curve of a brown shawl there looked out at him the strangest little red face with crumpled features, moist, loose lips, and eyelids which quivered like a rabbit's nostrils. The weak neck had let the head topple over, and it rested upon the shoulder.

"Kiss it, Robert!" cried the grandmother. "Kiss your son!"

But he felt a resentment to the little, red, blinking creature. He could not forgive it yet for that long night of misery. He caught sight of a white face in the bed and he ran towards it with such love and pity as his speech could find no words for.

"Thank God it is over! Lucy, dear, it was dreadful!"

"But I'm so happy now. I never was so happy in my life."

Her eyes were fixed upon the brown bundle.

"You mustn't talk," said Mrs. Peyton.

"But don't leave me," whispered his wife.

So he sat in silence with his hand in hers. The lamp was burning dim and the first cold light of dawn was breaking through the window. The night had been long and dark but the day was the sweeter and the purer in consequence. London was waking up. The roar began to rise from the street. Lives had come and lives had gone, but the great machine was still working out its dim and tragic destiny.

SWEETHEARTS.

It is hard for the general practitioner who sits among his patients both morning and evening, and sees them in their homes between, to steal time for one little daily breath of cleanly air. To win it he must slip early from his bed and walk out between shuttered shops when it is chill but very clear, and all things are sharply outlined, as in a frost. It is an hour that has a charm of its own, when, but for a postman or a milkman, one has the pavement to oneself, and even the most common thing takes an ever-recurring freshness, as though causeway, and lamp, and signboard had all wakened to the new day. Then even an inland city may seem beautiful, and bear virtue in its smoke-tainted air.

But it was by the sea that I lived, in a town that was unlovely enough were it not for its glorious neighbour. And who cares for the town when one can sit on the bench at the headland, and look out over the huge, blue bay, and the yellow scimitar that curves before it. I loved it when its great face was freckled with the fishing boats, and I loved it when the big ships went past, far out, a little hillock of white and no hull, with topsails curved like a bodice, so stately and demure. But most of all I loved it when no trace of man marred the majesty of Nature, and when the sun-bursts slanted down on it from between the drifting rainclouds. Then I have seen the further edge draped in the gauze of the driving rain, with its thin grey shading under the slow clouds, while my headland was golden, and the sun gleamed upon the breakers and struck deep through the green waves beyond, showing up the purple patches where the beds of seaweed are lying. Such a morning as that, with the wind in his hair, and the spray on his lips, and the cry of the eddying gulls in his ear, may send a man back braced afresh to the reek of a sick-room, and the dead, drab weariness of practice.

It was on such another day that I first saw my old man. He came to my bench just as I was leaving it. My eye must have picked him out even in a crowded street, for he was a man of large frame and fine presence, with something of distinction in the set of his lip and the poise of his head. He limped up the winding path leaning heavily upon his stick, as though those great shoulders had become too much at last for the failing limbs that bore them. As he approached, my eyes caught Nature's danger signal, that faint bluish tinge in nose and lip which tells of a labouring heart.

"The brae is a little trying, sir," said I. "Speaking as a physician, I should say that you would do well to rest here before you go further."

He inclined his head in a stately, old-world fashion, and seated himself upon the bench. Seeing that he had no wish to speak I was silent also, but I could not help watching him out of the corners of my eyes, for he was such a wonderful survival of the early half of the century, with his low-crowned, curly-brimmed hat, his black satin tie which fastened with a buckle at the back, and, above all, his large, fleshy, clean-shaven face shot with its mesh of wrinkles. Those eyes, ere they had grown dim, had looked out from the box-seat of mail coaches, and had seen the knots of navvies as they toiled on the brown embankments. Those lips had smiled over the first numbers of "Pickwick," and had gossiped of the promising young man who wrote them. The face itself was a seventy-year almanack, and every seam an entry upon it where public as well as private sorrow left its trace. That pucker on the forehead stood for the Mutiny, perhaps; that line of care for the Crimean winter, it may be; and that last little sheaf of wrinkles, as my fancy hoped, for the death of Gordon. And so, as I dreamed in my foolish way, the old gentleman with the shining stock was gone, and it was seventy years of a great nation's life that took shape before me on the headland in the morning.

But he soon brought me back to earth again. As he recovered his breath he took a letter out of his pocket, and, putting on a pair of horn-rimmed eye-glasses, he read it through very carefully. Without any design of playing the spy I could not help observing that it was in a woman's hand. When he had finished it he read it again, and then sat with the corners of his mouth drawn down and his eyes staring vacantly out over the bay, the most forlorn-looking old gentleman that ever I have seen. All that is kindly within me was set stirring by that wistful face, but I knew that he was in no humour for talk, and so, at last, with my breakfast and my patients calling me, I left him on the bench and started for home.

I never gave him another thought until the next morning, when, at the same hour, he turned up upon the headland, and shared the bench which I had been accustomed to look upon as my own. He bowed again before sitting down, but was no more inclined than formerly to enter into conversation. There had been a change in him during the last twenty-four hours, and all for the worse. The face seemed more heavy and more wrinkled, while that ominous venous tinge was more pronounced as he panted up the hill. The clean lines of his cheek and chin were marred by a day's growth of grey stubble, and his large, shapely head had lost something of the brave carriage which had struck me when first I glanced at him. He had a letter there, the same, or another, but still in a woman's hand, and over this he was moping and mumbling in his senile fashion, with his brow puckered, and the corners of his mouth drawn down like those of a fretting child. So I left him, with a vague wonder as to who he might be, and why a single spring day should have wrought such a change upon him.

So interested was I that next morning I was on the look out for him. Sure enough, at the same hour, I saw him coming up the hill; but very slowly, with a bent back and a heavy head. It was shocking to me to see the change in him as he approached.

"I am afraid that our air does not agree with you, sir," I ventured to remark.

But it was as though he had no heart for talk. He tried, as I thought, to make some fitting reply, but it slurred off into a mumble and silence. How bent and weak and old he seemed—ten years older at the least than when first I had seen him! It went to my heart to see this fine old fellow wasting away before my eyes. There was the eternal letter which he unfolded with his shaking fingers. Who was this woman whose words moved him so? Some daughter, perhaps, or granddaughter, who should have been the light of his home instead of—— I smiled to find how bitter I was growing, and how swiftly I was weaving a romance round an unshaven old man and his correspondence. Yet all day he lingered in my mind, and I had fitful glimpses of those two trembling, blue-veined, knuckly hands with the paper rustling between them.

I had hardly hoped to see him again. Another day's decline must, I thought, hold him to his room, if not to his bed. Great, then, was my surprise when, as I approached my bench, I saw that he was already there. But as I came up to him I could scarce be sure that it was indeed the same man. There were the curly-brimmed hat, and the shining stock, and the horn glasses, but where were the stoop and the grey-stubbled, pitiable face? He was clean-shaven and firm lipped, with a bright eye and a head that poised itself upon his great shoulders like an eagle on a rock. His back was as straight and square as a grenadier's, and he switched at the pebbles with his stick in his exuberant vitality. In the button-hole of his well-brushed black coat there glinted a golden blossom, and the corner of a dainty red silk handkerchief lapped over from his breast pocket. He might have been the eldest son of the weary creature who had sat there the morning before.

"Good morning, Sir, good morning!" he cried with a merry waggle of his cane.

"Good morning!" I answered, "how beautiful the bay is looking."

"Yes, Sir, but you should have seen it just before the sun rose."

"What, have you been here since then?"

"I was here when there was scarce light to see the path."

"You are a very early riser."

"On occasion, sir; on occasion!" He cocked his eye at me as if to gauge whether I were worthy of his confidence. "The fact is, sir, that my wife is coming back to me to day."

I suppose that my face showed that I did not quite see the force of the explanation. My eyes, too, may have given him assurance of sympathy, for he moved quite close to me and began speaking in a low, confidential voice, as if the matter were of such weight that even the sea-gulls must be kept out of our councils.

"Are you a married man, Sir?"

"No, I am not."

"Ah, then you cannot quite understand it. My wife and I have been married for nearly fifty years, and we have never been parted, never at all, until now."

"Was it for long?" I asked.

"Yes, sir. This is the fourth day. She had to go to Scotland. A matter of duty, you understand, and the doctors would not let me go. Not that I would have allowed them to stop me, but she was on their side. Now, thank God! it is over, and she may be here at any moment."

"Here!"

"Yes, here. This headland and bench were old friends of ours thirty years ago. The people with whom we stay are not, to tell the truth, very congenial, and we have, little privacy among them. That is why we prefer to meet here. I could not be sure which train would bring her, but if she had come by the very earliest she would have found me waiting."

"In that case——" said I, rising.

"No, sir, no," he entreated, "I beg that you will stay. It does not weary you, this domestic talk of mine?"

"On the contrary."

"I have been so driven inwards during these few last days! Ah, what a nightmare it has been! Perhaps it may seem strange to you that an old fellow like me should feel like this."

"It is charming."

"No credit to me, sir! There's not a man on this planet but would feel the same if he had the good fortune to be married to such a woman. Perhaps, because you see me like this, and hear me speak of our long life together, you conceive that she is old, too."

He laughed heartily, and his eyes twinkled at the humour of the idea.

"She's one of those women, you know, who have youth in their hearts, and so it can never be very far from their faces. To me she's just as she was when she first took my hand in hers in '45. A wee little bit stouter, perhaps, but then, if she had a fault as a girl, it was that she was a shade too slender. She was above me in station, you know—I a clerk, and she the daughter of my employer. Oh! it was quite a romance, I give you my word, and I won her; and, somehow, I have never got over the freshness and the wonder of it. To think that that sweet, lovely girl has walked by my side all through life, and that I have been able——"

He stopped suddenly, and I glanced round at him in surprise. He was shaking all over, in every fibre of his great body. His hands were clawing at the woodwork, and his feet shuffling on the gravel. I saw what it was. He was trying to rise, but was so excited that he could not. I half extended my hand, but a higher courtesy constrained me to draw it back again and turn my face to the sea. An instant afterwards he was up and hurrying down the path.

A woman was coming towards us. She was quite close before he had seen her —thirty yards at the utmost. I know not if she had ever been as he described her, or whether it was but some ideal which he carried in his brain. The person upon whom I looked was tall, it is true, but she was thick and shapeless, with a ruddy, full-blown face, and a skirt grotesquely gathered up. There was a green ribbon in her hat, which jarred upon my eyes, and her blouse-like bodice was full and clumsy. And this was the lovely girl, the ever youthful! My heart sank as I thought how little such a woman might appreciate him, how unworthy she might be of his love.

She came up the path in her solid way, while he staggered along to meet her. Then, as they came together, looking discreetly out of the furthest corner of my eye, I saw that he put out both his hands, while she, shrinking from a public caress, took one of them in hers and shook it. As she did so I saw her face, and I was easy in my mind for my old man. God grant that when this hand is shaking, and when this back is bowed, a woman's eyes may look so into mine.

A PHYSIOLOGIST'S WIFE.

Professor Ainslie Grey had not come down to breakfast at the usual hour. The presentation chiming-clock which stood between the terra-cotta busts of Claude Bernard and of John Hunter upon the dining-room mantelpiece had rung out the half-hour and the three-quarters. Now its golden hand was verging upon the nine, and yet there were no signs of the master of the house.

It was an unprecedented occurrence. During the twelve years that she had kept house for him, his youngest sister had never known him a second behind his time. She sat now in front of the high silver coffee-pot, uncertain whether to order the gong to be resounded or to wait on in silence. Either course might be a mistake. Her brother was not a man who permitted mistakes.

Miss Ainslie Grey was rather above the middle height, thin, with peering, puckered eyes, and the rounded shoulders which mark the bookish woman. Her face was long and spare, flecked with colour above the cheek-bones, with a reasonable, thoughtful forehead, and a dash of absolute obstinacy in her thin lips and prominent chin. Snow white cuffs and collar, with a plain dark dress, cut with almost Quaker-like simplicity, bespoke the primness of her taste. An ebony cross hung over her flattened chest. She sat very upright in her chair, listening with raised eyebrows, and swinging her eye-glasses backwards and forwards with a nervous gesture which was peculiar to her.

Suddenly she gave a sharp, satisfied jerk of the head, and began to pour out the coffee. From outside there came the dull thudding sound of heavy feet upon thick carpet. The door swung open, and the Professor entered with a quick, nervous step. He nodded to his sister, and seating himself at the other side of the table, began to open the small pile of letters which lay beside his plate.

Professor Ainslie Grey was at that time forty-three years of age—nearly twelve years older than his sister. His career had been a brilliant one. At Edinburgh, at Cambridge, and at Vienna he had laid the foundations of his great reputation, both in physiology and in zoology.

His pamphlet, On the Mesoblastic Origin of Excitomotor Nerve Roots, had won him his fellowship of the Royal Society; and his researches, Upon the Nature of Bathybius, with some Remarks upon Lithococci, had been translated into at least three European languages. He had been referred to by one of the greatest living authorities as being the very type and embodiment of all that was best in modern science. No wonder, then, that when the commercial city of Birchespool decided to create a medical school, they were only too glad to confer the chair of physiology upon Mr. Ainslie Grey. They valued him the more from the conviction that their class was only one step in his upward journey, and that the first vacancy would remove him to some more illustrious seat of learning.

In person he was not unlike his sister. The same eyes, the same contour, the same intellectual forehead. His lips, however, were firmer, and his long, thin, lower jaw was sharper and more decided. He ran his finger and thumb down it from time to time, as he glanced over his letters.

"Those maids are very noisy," he remarked, as a clack of tongues sounded in the distance.

"It is Sarah," said his sister; "I shall speak about it."

She had handed over his coffee-cup, and was sipping at her own, glancing furtively through her narrowed lids at the austere face of her brother.

"The first great advance of the human race," said the Professor, "was when, by the development of their left frontal convolutions, they attained the power of speech. Their second advance was when they learned to control that power. Woman has not yet attained the second stage."

He half closed his eyes as he spoke, and thrust his chin forward, but as he ceased he had a trick of suddenly opening both eyes very wide and staring sternly at his interlocutor.

"I am not garrulous, John," said his sister.

"No, Ada; in many respects you approach the superior or male type."

The Professor bowed over his egg with the manner of one who utters a courtly compliment; but the lady pouted, and gave an impatient little shrug of her shoulders.

"You were late this morning, John," she remarked, after a pause.

"Yes, Ada; I slept badly. Some little cerebral congestion, no doubt due to over-stimulation of the centers of thought. I have been a little disturbed in my mind."

His sister stared across at him in astonishment. The Professor's mental processes had hitherto been as regular as his habits. Twelve years' continual intercourse had taught her that he lived in a serene and rarefied atmosphere of scientific calm, high above the petty emotions which affect humbler minds.

"You are surprised, Ada," he remarked. "Well, I cannot wonder at it. I should have been surprised myself if I had been told that I was so sensitive to vascular influences. For, after all, all disturbances are vascular if you probe them deep enough. I am thinking of getting married."

"Not Mrs. O'James" cried Ada Grey, laying down her egg-spoon.

"My dear, you have the feminine quality of receptivity very remarkably developed. Mrs. O'James is the lady in question."

"But you know so little of her. The Esdailes themselves know so little. She is really only an acquaintance, although she is staying at The Lindens. Would it not be wise to speak to Mrs. Esdaile first, John?"

"I do not think, Ada, that Mrs. Esdaile is at all likely to say anything which would materially affect my course of action. I have given the matter due consideration. The scientific mind is slow at arriving at conclusions, but having once formed them, it is not prone to change. Matrimony is the natural condition of the human race. I have, as you know, been so engaged in academical and other work, that I have had no time to devote to merely personal questions. It is different now, and I see no valid reason why I should forego this opportunity of seeking a suitable helpmate."

"And you are engaged?"

"Hardly that, Ada. I ventured yesterday to indicate to the lady that I was prepared to submit to the common lot of humanity. I shall wait upon her after my morning lecture, and learn how far my proposals meet with her acquiescence. But you frown, Ada!"

His sister started, and made an effort to conceal her expression of annoyance.

She even stammered out some few words of congratulation, but a vacant look had come into her brother's eyes, and he was evidently not listening to her.

"I am sure, John, that I wish you the happiness which you deserve. If I hesitated at all, it is because I know how much is at stake, and because the thing is so sudden, so unexpected." Her thin white hand stole up to the black cross upon her bosom. "These are moments when we need guidance, John. If I could persuade you to turn to spiritual———"

The Professor waved the suggestion away with a deprecating hand.

"It is useless to reopen that question," he said. "We cannot argue upon it. You assume more than I can grant. I am forced to dispute your premises. We have no common basis."

His sister sighed.

"You have no faith," she said.

"I have faith in those great evolutionary forces which are leading the human race to some unknown but elevated goal."

"You believe in nothing."

"On the contrary, my dear Ada, I believe in the differentiation of protoplasm."

She shook her head sadly. It was the one subject upon which she ventured to dispute her brother's infallibility.

"This is rather beside the question," remarked the Professor, folding up his napkin. "If I am not mistaken, there is some possibility of another matrimonial event occurring in the family. Eh, Ada? What!"

His small eyes glittered with sly facetiousness as he shot a twinkle at his sister. She sat very stiff, and traced patterns upon the cloth with the sugar-tongs.

"Dr. James M'Murdo O'Brien———" said the Professor, sonorously.

"Don't, John, don't!" cried Miss Ainslie Grey.

"Dr. James M'Murdo O'Brien," continued her brother inexorably, "is a man who has already made his mark upon the science of the day. He is my first and my most distinguished pupil. I assure you, Ada, that his 'Remarks upon the Bile-Pigments, with special reference to Urobilin,' is likely to live as a classic. It is not too much to say that he has revolutionised our views about urobilin."

He paused, but his sister sat silent, with bent head and flushed cheeks. The little ebony cross rose and fell with her hurried breathings.

"Dr. James M'Murdo O'Brien has, as you know, the offer of the physiological chair at Melbourne. He has been in Australia five years, and has a brilliant future before him. To-day he leaves us for Edinburgh, and in two months' time, he goes out to take over his new duties. You know his feeling towards you. It, rests with you as to whether he goes out alone. Speaking for myself, I cannot imagine any higher mission for a woman of culture than to go through life in the company of a man who is capable of such a research as that which Dr. James M'Murdo O'Brien has brought to a successful conclusion."

"He has not spoken to me," murmured the lady.

"Ah, there are signs which are more subtle than speech," said her brother, wagging his head. "But you are pale. Your vasomotor system is excited. Your arterioles have contracted. Let me entreat you to compose yourself. I think I hear the carriage. I fancy that you may have a visitor this morning, Ada. You will excuse me now."

With a quick glance at the clock he strode off into the hall, and within a few minutes he was rattling in his quiet, well-appointed brougham through the brick-lined streets of Birchespool.

His lecture over, Professor Ainslie Grey paid a visit to his laboratory, where he adjusted several scientific instruments, made a note as to the progress of three separate infusions of bacteria, cut half-a-dozen sections with a microtome, and finally resolved the difficulties of seven different gentlemen, who were pursuing researches in as many separate lines of inquiry. Having thus conscientiously and methodically completed the routine of his duties, he returned to his carriage and ordered the coachman to drive him to The Lindens. His face as he drove was cold and impassive, but he drew his fingers from time to time down his prominent chin with a jerky, twitchy movement.

The Lindens was an old-fashioned, ivy-clad house which had once been in the country, but was now caught in the long, red-brick feelers of the growing city. It still stood back from the road in the privacy of its own grounds. A winding path, lined with laurel bushes, led to the arched and porticoed entrance. To the right was a lawn, and at the far side, under the shadow of a hawthorn, a lady sat in a garden-chair with a book in her hands. At the click of the gate she started, and the Professor, catching sight of her, turned away from the door, and strode in her direction.

"What! won't you go in and see Mrs. Esdaile?" she asked, sweeping out from under the shadow of the hawthorn.

She was a small woman, strongly feminine, from the rich coils of her light-coloured hair to the dainty garden slipper which peeped from under her cream-tinted dress. One tiny well-gloved hand was outstretched in greeting, while the other pressed a thick, green-covered volume against her side. Her decision and quick, tactful manner bespoke the mature woman of the world; but her upraised face had preserved a girlish and even infantile expression of innocence in its large, fearless, grey eyes, and sensitive, humorous mouth. Mrs. O'James was a widow, and she was two-and-thirty years of age; but neither fact could have been deduced from her appearance.

"You will surely go in and see Mrs. Esdaile," she repeated, glancing up at him with eyes which had in them something between a challenge and a caress.

"I did not come to see Mrs. Esdaile," he answered, with no relaxation of his cold and grave manner; "I came to see you."

"I am sure I should be highly honoured," she said, with just the slightest little touch of brogue in her accent. "What are the students to do without their Professor?"

"I have already completed my academic duties. Take my arm, and we shall walk in the sunshine. Surely we cannot wonder that Eastern people should have made a deity of the sun. It is the great beneficent force of Nature—man's ally against cold, sterility, and all that is abhorrent to him. What were you reading?"

"Hale's Matter and Life."

The Professor raised his thick eyebrows.

"Hale!" he said, and then again in a kind of whisper, "Hale!"

"You differ from him?" she asked.

"It is not I who differ from him. I am only a monad—a thing of no moment. The whole tendency of the highest plane of modern thought differs from him. He defends the indefensible. He is an excellent observer, but a feeble reasoner. I should not recommend you to found your conclusions upon Hale."

"I must read Nature's Chronicle to counteract his pernicious influence," said Mrs. O'James, with a soft, cooing laugh.

Nature's Chronicle was one of the many books in which Professor Ainslie Grey had enforced the negative doctrines of scientific agnosticism.

"It is a faulty work," said he; "I cannot recommend it. I would rather refer you to the standard writings of some of my older and more eloquent colleagues."

There was a pause in their talk as they paced up and down on the green, velvet-like lawn in the genial sunshine.

"Have you thought at all," he asked at last, "of the matter upon which I spoke to you last night?"

She said nothing, but walked by his side with her eyes averted and her face aslant.

"I would not hurry you unduly," he continued. "I know that it is a matter which can scarcely be decided off-hand. In my own case, it cost me some thought before I ventured to make the suggestion. I am not an emotional man, but I am conscious in your presence of the great evolutionary instinct which makes either sex the complement of the other."

"You believe in love, then?" she asked, with a twinkling, upward glance.

"I am forced to."

"And yet you can deny the soul?"

"How far these questions are psychic and how far material is still sub judice," said the Professor, with an air of toleration. "Protoplasm may prove to be the physical basis of love as well as of life."

"How inflexible you are!" she exclaimed; "you would draw love down to the level of physics."

"Or draw physics up to the level of love."

"Come, that is much better," she cried, with her sympathetic laugh. "That is really very pretty, and puts science in quite a delightful light."

Her eyes sparkled, and she tossed her chin with the pretty, wilful air of a woman who is mistress of the situation.

"I have reason to believe," said the Professor, "that my position here will prove to be only a stepping-stone to some wider scene of scientific activity. Yet, even here, my chair brings me in some fifteen hundred pounds a year, which is supplemented by a few hundreds from my books. I should therefore be in a position to provide you with those comforts to which you are accustomed. So much for my pecuniary position. As to my constitution, it has always been sound. I have never suffered from any illness in my life, save fleeting attacks of cephalalgia, the result of too prolonged a stimulation of the centres of cerebration. My father and mother had no sign of any morbid diathesis, but I will not conceal from you that my grandfather was afflicted with podagra."

Mrs. O'James looked startled.

"Is that very serious?" she asked.

"It is gout," said the Professor.

"Oh, is that all? It sounded much worse than that."

"It is a grave taint, but I trust that I shall not be a victim to atavism. I have laid these facts before you because they are factors which cannot be overlooked in forming your decision. May I ask now whether you see your way to accepting my proposal?"

He paused in his walk, and looked earnestly and expectantly down at her.

A struggle was evidently going on in her mind. Her eyes were cast down, her little slipper tapped the lawn, and her fingers played nervously with her chatelain. Suddenly, with a sharp, quick gesture which had in it something of ABANDON and recklessness, she held out her hand to her companion.

"I accept," she said.

They were standing under the shadow of the hawthorn. He stooped gravely down, and kissed her glove-covered fingers.

"I trust that you may never have cause to regret your decision," he said.

"I trust that you never may," she cried, with a heaving breast.

There were tears in her eyes, and her lips twitched with some strong emotion.

"Come into the sunshine again," said he. "It is the great restorative. Your nerves are shaken. Some little congestion of the medulla and pons. It is always instructive to reduce psychic or emotional conditions to their physical equivalents. You feel that your anchor is still firm in a bottom of ascertained fact."

"But it is so dreadfully unromantic," said Mrs. O'James, with her old twinkle.

"Romance is the offspring of imagination and of ignorance. Where science throws her calm, clear light there is happily no room for romance."

"But is not love romance?" she asked.

"Not at all. Love has been taken away from the poets, and has been brought within the domain of true science. It may prove to be one of the great cosmic elementary forces. When the atom of hydrogen draws the atom of chlorine towards it to form the perfected molecule of hydrochloric acid, the force which it exerts may be intrinsically similar to that which draws me to you. Attraction and repulsion appear to be the primary forces. This is attraction."

"And here is repulsion," said Mrs. O'James, as a stout, florid lady came sweeping across the lawn in their direction. "So glad you have come out, Mrs. Esdaile! Here is Professor Grey."

"How do you do, Professor?" said the lady, with some little pomposity of manner. "You were very wise to stay out here on so lovely a day. Is it not heavenly?"

"It is certainly very fine weather," the Professor answered.

"Listen to the wind sighing in the trees!" cried Mrs. Esdaile, holding up one finger. "It is Nature's lullaby. Could you not imagine it, Professor Grey, to be the whisperings of angels?"

"The idea had not occurred to me, madam."

"Ah, Professor, I have always the same complaint against you. A want of rapport with the deeper meanings of nature. Shall I say a want of imagination. You do not feel an emotional thrill at the singing of that thrush?"

"I confess that I am not conscious of one, Mrs. Esdaile."

"Or at the delicate tint of that background of leaves? See the rich greens!"

"Chlorophyll," murmured the Professor.

"Science is so hopelessly prosaic. It dissects and labels, and loses sight of the great things in its attention to the little ones. You have a poor opinion of woman's intellect, Professor Grey. I think that I have heard you say so."

"It is a question of avoirdupois," said the Professor, closing his eyes and shrugging his shoulders. "The female cerebrum averages two ounces less in weight than the male. No doubt there are exceptions. Nature is always elastic."

"But the heaviest thing is not always the strongest," said Mrs. O'James, laughing. "Isn't there a law of compensation in science? May we not hope to make up in quality for what we lack in quantity?"

"I think not," remarked the Professor, gravely. "But there is your luncheon-gong. No, thank you, Mrs. Esdaile, I cannot stay. My carriage is waiting. Good-bye. Good-bye, Mrs. O'James."

He raised his hat and stalked slowly away among the laurel bushes.

"He has no taste," said Mrs. Esdaile—"no eye for beauty."

"On the contrary," Mrs. O'James answered, with a saucy little jerk of the chin. "He has just asked me to be his wife."

As Professor Ainslie Grey ascended the steps of his house, the hall-door opened and a dapper gentleman stepped briskly out. He was somewhat sallow in the face, with dark, beady eyes, and a short, black beard with an aggressive bristle. Thought and work had left their traces upon his face, but he moved with the brisk activity of a man who had not yet bade good-bye to his youth.

"I'm in luck's way," he cried. "I wanted to see you."

"Then come back into the library," said the Professor; "you must stay and have lunch with us."

The two men entered the hall, and the Professor led the way into his private sanctum. He motioned his companion into an arm-chair.

"I trust that you have been successful, O'Brien," said he. "I should be loath to exercise any undue pressure upon my sister Ada; but I have given her to understand that there is no one whom I should prefer for a brother-in-law to my most brilliant scholar, the author of Some Remarks upon the Bile-Pigments, with special reference to Urobilin."

"You are very kind, Professor Grey—you have always been very kind," said the other. "I approached Miss Grey upon the subject; she did not say No."

"She said Yes, then?"

"No; she proposed to leave the matter open until my return from Edinburgh. I go to-day, as you know, and I hope to commence my research to-morrow."

"On the comparative anatomy of the vermiform appendix, by James M'Murdo O'Brien," said the Professor, sonorously. "It is a glorious subject—a subject which lies at the very root of evolutionary philosophy."

"Ah! she is the dearest girl," cried O'Brien, with a sudden little spurt of Celtic enthusiasm—"she is the soul of truth and of honour."

"The vermiform appendix——" began the Professor.

"She is an angel from heaven," interrupted the other. "I fear that it is my advocacy of scientific freedom in religious thought which stands in my way with her."

"You must not truckle upon that point. You must be true to your convictions; let there be no compromise there."

"My reason is true to agnosticism, and yet I am conscious of a void—a vacuum. I had feelings at the old church at home between the scent of the incense and the roll of the organ, such as I have never experienced in the laboratory or the lecture-room."

"Sensuous-purely sensuous," said the Professor, rubbing his chin. "Vague hereditary tendencies stirred into life by the stimulation of the nasal and auditory nerves."

"Maybe so, maybe so," the younger man answered thoughtfully. "But this was not what I wished to speak to you about. Before I enter your family, your sister and you have a claim to know all that I can tell you about my career. Of my worldly prospects I have already spoken to you. There is only one point which I have omitted to mention. I am a widower."

The Professor raised his eyebrows.

"This is news indeed," said he.

"I married shortly after my arrival in Australia. Miss Thurston was her name. I met her in society. It was a most unhappy match."

Some painful emotion possessed him. His quick, expressive features quivered, and his white hands tightened upon the arms of the chair. The Professor turned away towards the window.

"You are the best judge," he remarked "but I should not think that it was necessary to go into details."

"You have a right to know everything—you and Miss Grey. It is not a matter on which I can well speak to her direct. Poor Jinny was the best of women, but she was open to flattery, and liable to be misled by designing persons. She was untrue to me, Grey. It is a hard thing to say of the dead, but she was untrue to me. She fled to Auckland with a man whom she had known before her marriage. The brig which carried them foundered, and not a soul was saved."

"This is very painful, O'Brien," said the Professor, with a deprecatory motion of his hand. "I cannot see, however, how it affects your relation to my sister."

"I have eased my conscience," said O'Brien, rising from his chair; "I have told you all that there is to tell. I should not like the story to reach you through any lips but my own."

"You are right, O'Brien. Your action has been most honourable and considerate. But you are not to blame in the matter, save that perhaps you showed a little precipitancy in choosing a life-partner without due care and inquiry."

O'Brien drew his hand across his eyes.

"Poor girl!" he cried. "God help me, I love her still! But I must go."

"You will lunch with us?"

"No, Professor; I have my packing still to do. I have already bade Miss Grey adieu. In two months I shall see you again."

"You will probably find me a married man."

"Married!"

"Yes, I have been thinking of it."

"My dear Professor, let me congratulate you with all my heart. I had no idea. Who is the lady?"

"Mrs. O'James is her name—a widow of the same nationality as yourself. But to return to matters of importance, I should be very happy to see the proofs of your paper upon the vermiform appendix. I may be able to furnish you with material for a footnote or two."

"Your assistance will be invaluable to me," said O'Brien, with enthusiasm, and the two men parted in the hall. The Professor walked back into the dining-room, where his sister was already seated at the luncheon-table.

"I shall be married at the registrar's," he remarked; "I should strongly recommend you to do the same."

Professor Ainslie Grey was as good as his word. A fortnight's cessation of his classes gave him an opportunity which was too good to let pass. Mrs. O'James was an orphan, without relations and almost without friends in the country. There was no obstacle in the way of a speedy wedding. They were married, accordingly, in the quietest manner possible, and went off to Cambridge together, where the Professor and his charming wife were present at several academic observances, and varied the routine of their honeymoon by incursions into biological laboratories and medical libraries. Scientific friends were loud in their congratulations, not only upon Mrs. Grey's beauty, but upon the unusual quickness and intelligence which she displayed in discussing physiological questions. The Professor was himself astonished at the accuracy of her information. "You have a remarkable range of knowledge for a woman, Jeannette," he remarked upon more than one occasion. He was even prepared to admit that her cerebrum might be of the normal weight.

One foggy, drizzling morning they returned to Birchespool, for the next day would re-open the session, and Professor Ainslie Grey prided himself upon having never once in his life failed to appear in his lecture-room at the very stroke of the hour. Miss Ada Grey welcomed them with a constrained cordiality, and handed over the keys of office to the new mistress. Mrs. Grey pressed her warmly to remain, but she explained that she had already accepted an invitation which would engage her for some months. The same evening she departed for the south of England.

A couple of days later the maid carried a card just after breakfast into the library where the Professor sat revising his morning lecture. It announced the re-arrival of Dr. James M'Murdo O'Brien. Their meeting was effusively genial on the part of the younger man, and coldly precise on that of his former teacher.

"You see there have been changes," said the Professor.

"So I heard. Miss Grey told me in her letters, and I read the notice in the British Medical Journal. So it's really married you are. How quickly and quietly you have managed it all!"

"I am constitutionally averse to anything in the nature of show or ceremony. My wife is a sensible woman—I may even go the length of saying that, for a woman, she is abnormally sensible. She quite agreed with me in the course which I have adopted."

"And your research on Vallisneria?"

"This matrimonial incident has interrupted it, but I have resumed my classes, and we shall soon be quite in harness again."

"I must see Miss Grey before I leave England. We have corresponded, and I think that all will be well. She must come out with me. I don't think I could go without her."

The Professor shook his head.

"Your nature is not so weak as you pretend," he said. "Questions of this sort are, after all, quite subordinate to the great duties of life."

O'Brien smiled.

"You would have me take out my Celtic soul and put in a Saxon one," he said. "Either my brain is too small or my heart is too big. But when may I call and pay my respects to Mrs. Grey? Will she be at home this afternoon?"

"She is at home now. Come into the morning-room. She will be glad to make your acquaintance."

They walked across the linoleum-paved hall. The Professor opened the door of the room, and walked in, followed by his friend. Mrs. Grey was sitting in a basket-chair by the window, light and fairy-like in a loose-flowing, pink morning-gown. Seeing a visitor, she rose and swept towards them. The Professor heard a dull thud behind him. O'Brien had fallen back into a chair, with his hand pressed tight to his side.

"Jinny!" he gasped—"Jinny!"

Mrs. Grey stopped dead in her advance, and stared at him with a face from which every expression had been struck out, save one of astonishment and horror. Then with a sharp intaking of the breath she reeled, and would have fallen had the Professor not thrown his long, nervous arm round her.

"Try this sofa," said he.

She sank back among the cushions with the same white, cold, dead look upon her face. The Professor stood with his back to the empty fireplace and glanced from the one to the other.

"So, O'Brien," he said at last, "you have already made the acquaintance of my wife!"

"Your wife," cried his friend hoarsely. "She is no wife of yours. God help me, she is MY wife."

The Professor stood rigidly upon the hearthrug. His long, thin fingers were intertwined, and his head sunk a little forward. His two companions had eyes only for each other.

"Jinny!" said he.

"James!"

"How could you leave me so, Jinny? How could you have the heart to do it? I thought you were dead. I mourned for your death—ay, and you have made me mourn for you living. You have withered my life."

She made no answer, but lay back among her cushions with her eyes still fixed upon him.

"Why do you not speak?"

"Because you are right, James. I HAVE treated you cruelly—shamefully. But it is not as bad as you think."

"You fled with De Horta."

"No, I did not. At the last moment my better nature prevailed. He went alone. But I was ashamed to come back after what I had written to you. I could not face you. I took passage alone to England under a new name, and here I have lived ever since. It seemed to me that I was beginning life again. I knew that you thought I was drowned. Who could have dreamed that fate would throw us together again! When the Professor asked me——"

She stopped and gave a gasp for breath.

"You are faint," said the Professor—"keep the head low; it aids the cerebral circulation." He flattened down the cushion. "I am sorry to leave you, O'Brien; but I have my class duties to look to. Possibly I may find you here when I return."

With a grim and rigid face he strode out of the room. Not one of the three hundred students who listened to his lecture saw any change in his manner and appearance, or could have guessed that the austere gentleman in front of them had found out at last how hard it is to rise above one's humanity. The lecture over, he performed his routine duties in the laboratory, and then drove back to his own house. He did not enter by the front door, but passed through the garden to the folding glass casement which led out of the morning-room. As he approached he heard his wife's voice and O'Brien's in loud and animated talk. He paused among the rose-bushes, uncertain whether to interrupt them or no. Nothing was further from his nature than play the eavesdropper; but as he stood, still hesitating, words fell upon his ear which struck him rigid and motionless.

"You are still my wife, Jinny," said O'Brien; "I forgive you from the bottom of my heart. I love you, and I have never ceased to love you, though you had forgotten me."

"No, James, my heart was always in Melbourne. I have always been yours. I thought that it was better for you that I should seem to be dead."

"You must choose between us now, Jinny. If you determine to remain here, I shall not open my lips. There shall be no scandal. If, on the other hand, you come with me, it's little I care about the world's opinion. Perhaps I am as much to blame as you. I thought too much of my work and too little of my wife."

The Professor heard the cooing, caressing laugh which he knew so well.

"I shall go with you, James," she said.

"And the Professor——?"

"The poor Professor! But he will not mind much, James; he has no heart."

"We must tell him our resolution."

"There is no need," said Professor Ainslie Grey, stepping in through the open casement. "I have overheard the latter part of your conversation. I hesitated to interrupt you before you came to a conclusion."

O'Brien stretched out his hand and took that of the woman. They stood together with the sunshine on their faces. The Professor paused at the casement with his hands behind his back, and his long black shadow fell between them.

"You have come to a wise decision," said he. "Go back to Australia together, and let what has passed be blotted out of your lives."

"But you—you——" stammered O'Brien.

The Professor waved his hand.

"Never trouble about me," he said.

The woman gave a gasping cry.

"What can I do or say?" she wailed. "How could I have foreseen this? I thought my old life was dead. But it has come back again, with all its hopes and its desires. What can I say to you, Ainslie? I have brought shame and disgrace upon a worthy man. I have blasted your life. How you must hate and loathe me! I wish to God that I had never been born!"

"I neither hate nor loathe you, Jeannette," said the Professor, quietly. "You are wrong in regretting your birth, for you have a worthy mission before you in aiding the life-work of a man who has shown himself capable of the highest order of scientific research. I cannot with justice blame you personally for what has occurred. How far the individual monad is to be held responsible for hereditary and engrained tendencies, is a question upon which science has not yet said her last word."

He stood with his finger-tips touching, and his body inclined as one who is gravely expounding a difficult and impersonal subject. O'Brien had stepped forward to say something, but the other's attitude and manner froze the words upon his lips. Condolence or sympathy would be an impertinence to one who could so easily merge his private griefs in broad questions of abstract philosophy.

"It is needless to prolong the situation," the Professor continued, in the same measured tones. "My brougham stands at the door. I beg that you will use it as your own. Perhaps it would be as well that you should leave the town without unnecessary delay. Your things, Jeannette, shall be forwarded."

O'Brien hesitated with a hanging head.

"I hardly dare offer you my hand," he said.

"On the contrary. I think that of the three of us you come best out of the affair. You have nothing to be ashamed of."

"Your sister——"

"I shall see that the matter is put to her in its true light. Good-bye! Let me have a copy of your recent research. Good-bye, Jeannette!"

"Good-bye!"

Their hands met, and for one short moment their eyes also. It was only a glance, but for the first and last time the woman's intuition cast a light for itself into the dark places of a strong man's soul. She gave a little gasp, and her other hand rested for an instant, as white and as light as thistle-down, upon his shoulder.

"James, James!" she cried. "Don't you see that he is stricken to the heart?"

He turned her quietly away from him.

"I am not an emotional man," he said. "I have my duties—my research on

Vallisneria. The brougham is there. Your cloak is in the hall. Tell John where you wish to be driven. He will bring you anything you need. Now go."

His last two words were so sudden, so volcanic, in such contrast to his measured voice and mask-like face, that they swept the two away from him. He closed the door behind them and paced slowly up and down the room. Then he passed into the library and looked out over the wire blind. The carriage was rolling away. He caught a last glimpse of the woman who had been his wife. He saw the feminine droop of her head, and the curve of her beautiful throat.

Under some foolish, aimless impulse, he took a few quick steps towards the door. Then he turned, and throwing himself into his study-chair he plunged back into his work.

There was little scandal about this singular domestic incident. The Professor had few personal friends, and seldom went into society. His marriage had been so quiet that most of his colleagues had never ceased to regard him as a bachelor. Mrs. Esdaile and a few others might talk, but their field for gossip was limited, for they could only guess vaguely at the cause of this sudden separation.

The Professor was as punctual as ever at his classes, and as zealous in directing the laboratory work of those who studied under him. His own private researches were pushed on with feverish energy. It was no uncommon thing for his servants, when they came down of a morning, to hear the shrill scratchings of his tireless pen, or to meet him on the staircase as he ascended, grey and silent, to his room. In vain his friends assured him that such a life must undermine his health. He lengthened his hours until day and night were one long, ceaseless task.

Gradually under this discipline a change came over his appearance. His features, always inclined to gauntness, became even sharper and more pronounced. There were deep lines about his temples and across his brow. His cheek was sunken and his complexion bloodless. His knees gave under him when he walked; and once when passing out of his lecture-room he fell and had to be assisted to his carriage.

This was just before the end of the session and soon after the holidays commenced the professors who still remained in Birchespool were shocked to hear that their brother of the chair of physiology had sunk so low that no hopes could be entertained of his recovery. Two eminent physicians had consulted over his case without being able to give a name to the affection from which he suffered. A steadily decreasing vitality appeared to be the only symptom—a bodily weakness which left the mind unclouded. He was much interested himself in his own case, and made notes of his subjective sensations as an aid to diagnosis. Of his approaching end he spoke in his usual unemotional and somewhat pedantic fashion. "It is the assertion," he said, "of the liberty of the individual cell as opposed to the cell-commune. It is the dissolution of a co-operative society. The process is one of great interest."

And so one grey morning his co-operative society dissolved. Very quietly and softly he sank into his eternal sleep. His two physicians felt some slight embarrassment when called upon to fill in his certificate.

"It is difficult to give it a name," said one.

"Very," said the other.

"If he were not such an unemotional man, I should have said that he had died from some sudden nervous shock—from, in fact, what the vulgar would call a broken heart."

"I don't think poor Grey was that sort of a man at all."

"Let us call it cardiac, anyhow," said the older physician.

So they did so.

THE CASE OF LADY SANNOX.

The relations between Douglas Stone and the notorious Lady Sannox were very well known both among the fashionable circles of which she was a brilliant member, and the scientific bodies which numbered him among their most illustrious confreres. There was naturally, therefore, a very widespread interest when it was announced one morning that the lady had absolutely and for ever taken the veil, and that the world would see her no more. When, at the very tail of this rumour, there came the assurance that the celebrated operating surgeon, the man of steel nerves, had been found in the morning by his valet, seated on one side of his bed, smiling pleasantly upon the universe, with both legs jammed into one side of his breeches and his great brain about as valuable as a cap full of porridge, the matter was strong enough to give quite a little thrill of interest to folk who had never hoped that their jaded nerves were capable of such a sensation.

Douglas Stone in his prime was one of the most remarkable men in England. Indeed, he could hardly be said to have ever reached his prime, for he was but nine-and-thirty at the time of this little incident. Those who knew him best were aware that, famous as he was as a surgeon, he might have succeeded with even greater rapidity in any of a dozen lines of life. He could have cut his way to fame as a soldier, struggled to it as an explorer, bullied for it in the courts, or built it out of stone and iron as an engineer. He was born to be great, for he could plan what another man dare not do, and he could do what another man dare not plan. In surgery none could follow him. His nerve, his judgment, his intuition, were things apart. Again and again his knife cut away death, but grazed the very springs of life in doing it, until his assistants were as white as the patient. His energy, his audacity, his full-blooded self-confidence—does not the memory of them still linger to the south of Marylebone Road and the north of Oxford Street?

His vices were as magnificent as his virtues, and infinitely more picturesque. Large as was his income, and it was the third largest of all professional men in London, it was far beneath the luxury of his living. Deep in his complex nature lay a rich vein of sensualism, at the sport of which he placed all the prizes of his life. The eye, the ear, the touch, the palate—all were his masters. The bouquet of old vintages, the scent of rare exotics, the curves and tints of the daintiest potteries of Europe—it was to these that the quick-running stream of gold was transformed. And then there came his sudden mad passion for Lady Sannox, when a single interview with two challenging glances and a whispered word set him ablaze. She was the loveliest woman in London, and the only one to him. He was one of the handsomest men in London, but not the only one to her. She had a liking for new experiences, and was gracious to most men who wooed her. It may have been cause or it may have been effect that Lord Sannox looked fifty, though he was but six-and-thirty.

He was a quiet, silent, neutral-tinted man, this lord, with thin lips and heavy eyelids, much given to gardening, and full of home-like habits. He had at one time been fond of acting, had even rented a theatre in London, and on its boards had first seen Miss Marion Dawson, to whom he had offered his hand, his title, and the third of a county. Since his marriage this early hobby had become distasteful to him. Even in private theatricals it was no longer possible to persuade him to exercise the talent which he had often shown that he possessed. He was happier with a spud and a watering-can among his orchids and chrysanthemums.

It was quite an interesting problem whether he was absolutely devoid of sense, or miserably wanting in spirit. Did he know his lady's ways and condone them, or was he a mere blind, doting fool? It was a point to be discussed over the teacups in snug little drawing-rooms, or with the aid of a cigar in the bow windows of clubs. Bitter and plain were the comments among men upon his conduct. There was but one who had a good word to say for him, and he was the most silent member in the smoking-room. He had seen him break in a horse at the university, and it seemed to have left an impression upon his mind.

But when Douglas Stone became the favourite, all doubts as to Lord Sannox's knowledge or ignorance were set for ever at rest. There, was no subterfuge about Stone. In his high-handed, impetuous fashion, he set all caution and discretion at defiance. The scandal became notorious. A learned body intimated that his name had been struck from the list of its vice-presidents. Two friends implored him to consider his professional credit. He cursed them all three, and spent forty guineas on a bangle to take with him to the lady. He was at her house every evening, and she drove in his carriage in the afternoons. There was not an attempt on either side to conceal their relations; but there came at last a little incident to interrupt them.

It was a dismal winter's night, very cold and gusty, with the wind whooping in the chimneys and blustering against the window-panes. A thin spatter of rain tinkled on the glass with each fresh sough of the gale, drowning for the instant the dull gurgle and drip from the eves. Douglas Stone had finished his dinner, and sat by his fire in the study, a glass of rich port upon the malachite table at his elbow. As he raised it to his lips, he held it up against the lamplight, and watched with the eye of a connoisseur the tiny scales of beeswing which floated in its rich ruby depths. The fire, as it spurted up, threw fitful lights upon his bold, clear-cut face, with its widely-opened grey eyes, its thick and yet firm lips, and the deep, square jaw, which had something Roman in its strength and its animalism. He smiled from time to time as he nestled back in his luxurious chair. Indeed, he had a right to feel well pleased, for, against the advice of six colleagues, he had performed an operation that day of which only two cases were on record, and the result had been brilliant beyond all expectation. No other man in London would have had the daring to plan, or the skill to execute, such a heroic measure.

But he had promised Lady Sannox to see her that evening and it was already half-past eight. His hand was outstretched to the bell to order the carriage when he heard the dull thud of the knocker. An instant later there was the shuffling of feet in the hall, and the sharp closing of a door.

"A patient to see you, sir, in the consulting-room, said the butler.

"About himself?"

"No, sir; I think he wants you to go out."

"It is too late," cried Douglas Stone peevishly. "I won't go."

"This is his card, sir."

The butler presented it upon the gold salver which had been given to his master by the wife of a Prime Minister.

"'Hamil Ali, Smyrna.' Hum! The fellow is a Turk, I suppose."

"Yes, sir. He seems as if he came from abroad, sir. And he's in a terrible way."

"Tut, tut! I have an engagement. I must go somewhere else. But I'll see him. Show him in here, Pim."

A few moments later the butler swung open the door and ushered in a small and decrepit man, who walked with a bent back and with the forward push of the face and blink of the eyes which goes with extreme short sight. His face was swarthy, and his hair and beard of the deepest black. In one hand he held a turban of white muslin striped with red, in the other a small chamois leather bag.

"Good-evening," said Douglas Stone, when the butler had closed the door. "You speak English, I presume?"

"Yes, sir. I am from Asia Minor, but I speak English when I speak slow."

"You wanted me to go out, I understand?"

"Yes, sir. I wanted very much that you should see my wife."

"I could come in the morning, but I have an engagement which prevents me from seeing your wife to-night."

The Turk's answer was a singular one. He pulled the string which closed the mouth of the chamois leather bag, and poured a flood of gold on to the table.

"There are one hundred pounds there," said he, "and I promise you that it will not take you an hour. I have a cab ready at the door."

Douglas Stone glanced at his watch. An hour would not make it too late to visit Lady Sannox. He had been there later. And the fee was an extraordinarily high one. He had been pressed by his creditors lately, and he could not afford to let such a chance pass. He would go.

"What is the case?" he asked.

"Oh, it is so sad a one! So sad a one! You have not, perhaps, heard of the daggers of the Almohades?"

"Never."

"Ah, they are Eastern daggers of a great age and of a singular shape, with the hilt like what you call a stirrup. I am a curiosity dealer, you understand, and that is why I have come to England from Smyrna, but next week I go back once more. Many things I brought with me, and I have a few things left, but among them, to my sorrow, is one of these daggers."

"You will remember that I have an appointment, sir," said the surgeon, with some irritation. "Pray confine yourself to the necessary details."

"You will see that it is necessary. To-day my wife fell down in a faint in the room in which I keep my wares, and she cut her lower lip upon this cursed dagger of Almohades."

"I see," said Douglas Stone, rising. "And you wish me to dress the wound?"

"No, no, it is worse than that."

"What then?"

"These daggers are poisoned."

"Poisoned!"

"Yes, and there is no man, East or West, who can tell now what is the poison or what the cure. But all that is known I know, for my father was in this trade before me, and we have had much to do with these poisoned weapons."

"What are the symptoms?"

"Deep sleep, and death in thirty hours."

"And you say there is no cure. Why then should you pay me this considerable fee?"

"No drug can cure, but the knife may."

"And how?"

"The poison is slow of absorption. It remains for hours in the wound."

"Washing, then, might cleanse it?"

"No more than in a snake-bite. It is too subtle and too deadly."

"Excision of the wound, then?"

"That is it. If it be on the finger, take the finger off. So said my father always. But think of where this wound is, and that it is my wife. It is dreadful!"

But familiarity with such grim matters may take the finer edge from a man's sympathy. To Douglas Stone this was already an interesting case, and he brushed aside as irrelevant the feeble objections of the husband.

"It appears to be that or nothing," said he brusquely. "It is better to lose a lip than a life."

"Ah, yes, I know that you are right. Well, well, it is kismet, and must be faced. I have the cab, and you will come with me and do this thing."

Douglas Stone took his case of bistouries from a drawer, and placed it with a roll of bandage and a compress of lint in his pocket. He must waste no more time if he were to see Lady Sannox.

"I am ready," said he, pulling on his overcoat. "Will you take a glass of wine before you go out into this cold air?"

His visitor shrank away, with a protesting hand upraised.

"You forget that I am a Mussulman, and a true follower of the Prophet," said he. "But tell me what is the bottle of green glass which you have placed in your pocket?"

"It is chloroform."

"Ah, that also is forbidden to us. It is a spirit, and we make no use of such things."

"What! You would allow your wife to go through an operation without an anaesthetic?"

"Ah! she will feel nothing, poor soul. The deep sleep has already come on, which is the first working of the poison. And then I have given her of our Smyrna opium. Come, sir, for already an hour has passed."

As they stepped out into the darkness, a sheet of rain was driven in upon their faces, and the hall lamp, which dangled from the arm of a marble caryatid, went out with a fluff. Pim, the butler, pushed the heavy door to, straining hard with his shoulder against the wind, while the two men groped their way towards the yellow glare which showed where the cab was waiting. An instant later they were rattling upon their journey.

"Is it far?" asked Douglas Stone.

"Oh, no. We have a very little quiet place off the Euston Road."

The surgeon pressed the spring of his repeater and listened to the little tings which told him the hour. It was a quarter past nine. He calculated the distances, and the short time which it would take him to perform so trivial an operation. He ought to reach Lady Sannox by ten o'clock. Through the fogged windows he saw the blurred gas-lamps dancing past, with occasionally the broader glare of a shop front. The rain was pelting and rattling upon the leathern top of the carriage and the wheels swashed as they rolled through puddle and mud. Opposite to him the white headgear of his companion gleamed faintly through the obscurity. The surgeon felt in his pockets and arranged his needles, his ligatures and his safety-pins, that no time might be wasted when they arrived. He chafed with impatience and drummed his foot upon the floor.

But the cab slowed down at last and pulled up. In an instant Douglas Stone was out, and the Smyrna merchant's toe was at his very heel.

"You can wait," said he to the driver.

It was a mean-looking house in a narrow and sordid street. The surgeon, who knew his London well, cast a swift glance into the shadows, but there was nothing distinctive—no shop, no movement, nothing but a double line of dull, flat-faced houses, a double stretch of wet flagstones which gleamed in the lamplight, and a double rush of water in the gutters which swirled and gurgled towards the sewer gratings. The door which faced them was blotched and discoloured, and a faint light in the fan pane above it served to show the dust and the grime which covered it. Above, in one of the bedroom windows, there was a dull yellow glimmer. The merchant knocked loudly, and, as he turned his dark face towards the light, Douglas Stone could see that it was contracted with anxiety. A bolt was drawn, and an elderly woman with a taper stood in the doorway, shielding the thin flame with her gnarled hand.

"Is all well?" gasped the merchant.

"She is as you left her, sir."

"She has not spoken?"

"No; she is in a deep sleep."

The merchant closed the door, and Douglas Stone walked down the narrow passage, glancing about him in some surprise as he did so. There was no oilcloth, no mat, no hat-rack. Deep grey dust and heavy festoons of cobwebs met his eyes everywhere. Following the old woman up the winding stair, his firm footfall echoed harshly through the silent house. There was no carpet.

The bedroom was on the second landing. Douglas Stone followed the old nurse into it, with the merchant at his heels. Here, at least, there was furniture and to spare. The floor was littered and the corners piled with Turkish cabinets, inlaid tables, coats of chain mail, strange pipes, and grotesque weapons. A single small lamp stood upon a bracket on the wall. Douglas Stone took it down, and picking his way among the lumber, walked over to a couch in the corner, on which lay a woman dressed in the Turkish fashion, with yashmak and veil. The lower part of the face was exposed, and the surgeon saw a jagged cut which zigzagged along the border of the under lip.

"You will forgive the yashmak," said the Turk. "You know our views about woman in the East."

But the surgeon was not thinking about the yashmak. This was no longer a woman to him. It was a case. He stooped and examined the wound carefully.

"There are no signs of irritation," said he. "We might delay the operation until local symptoms develop."

The husband wrung his hands in incontrollable agitation.

"Oh! sir, sir!" he cried. "Do not trifle. You do not know. It is deadly. I know, and I give you my assurance that an operation is absolutely necessary. Only the knife can save her."

"And yet I am inclined to wait," said Douglas Stone.

"That is enough!" the Turk cried, angrily. "Every minute is of importance, and I cannot stand here and see my wife allowed to sink. It only remains for me to give you my thanks for having come, and to call in some other surgeon before it is too late."

Douglas Stone hesitated. To refund that hundred pounds was no pleasant matter. But of course if he left the case he must return the money. And if the Turk were right and the woman died, his position before a coroner might be an embarrassing one.

"You have had personal experience of this poison?" he asked.

"I have."

"And you assure me that an operation is needful."

"I swear it by all that I hold sacred."

"The disfigurement will be frightful."

"I can understand that the mouth will not be a pretty one to kiss."

Douglas Stone turned fiercely upon the man. The speech was a brutal one. But the Turk has his own fashion of talk and of thought, and there was no time for wrangling. Douglas Stone drew a bistoury from his case, opened it and felt the keen straight edge with his forefinger. Then he held the lamp closer to the bed. Two dark eyes were gazing up at him through the slit in the yashmak. They were all iris, and the pupil was hardly to be seen.

"You have given her a very heavy dose of opium."

"Yes, she has had a good dose."

He glanced again at the dark eyes which looked straight at his own. They were dull and lustreless, but, even as he gazed, a little shifting sparkle came into them, and the lips quivered.

"She is not absolutely unconscious," said he.

"Would it not be well to use the knife while it would be painless?"

The same thought had crossed the surgeon's mind. He grasped the wounded lip with his forceps, and with two swift cuts he took out a broad V-shaped piece. The woman sprang up on the couch with a dreadful gurgling scream. Her covering was torn from her face. It was a face that he knew. In spite of that protruding upper lip and that slobber of blood, it was a face that he knew. She kept on putting her hand up to the gap and screaming. Douglas Stone sat down at the foot of the couch with his knife and his forceps. The room was whirling round, and he had felt something go like a ripping seam behind his ear. A bystander would have said that his face was the more ghastly of the two. As in a dream, or as if he had been looking at something at the play, he was conscious that the Turk's hair and beard lay upon the table, and that Lord Sannox was leaning against the wall with his hand to his side, laughing silently. The screams had died away now, and the dreadful head had dropped back again upon the pillow, but Douglas Stone still sat motionless, and Lord Sannox still chuckled quietly to himself.

"It was really very necessary for Marion, this operation," said he, "not physically, but morally, you know, morally."

Douglas Stone stooped forwards and began to play with the fringe of the coverlet. His knife tinkled down upon the ground, but he still held the forceps and something more.

"I had long intended to make a little example," said Lord Sannox, suavely. "Your note of Wednesday miscarried, and I have it here in my pocket-book. I took some pains in carrying out my idea. The wound, by the way, was from nothing more dangerous than my signet ring."

He glanced keenly at his silent companion, and cocked the small revolver which he held in his coat pocket. But Douglas Stone was still picking at the coverlet.

"You see you have kept your appointment after all," said Lord Sannox.

And at that Douglas Stone began to laugh. He laughed long and loudly. But Lord Sannox did not laugh now. Something like fear sharpened and hardened his features. He walked from the room, and he walked on tiptoe. The old woman was waiting outside.

"Attend to your mistress when she awakes," said Lord Sannox.

Then he went down to the street. The cab was at the door, and the driver raised his hand to his hat.

"John," said Lord Sannox, "you will take the doctor home first. He will want leading downstairs, I think. Tell his butler that he has been taken ill at a case."

"Very good, sir."

"Then you can take Lady Sannox home."

"And how about yourself, sir?"

"Oh, my address for the next few months will be Hotel di Roma, Venice. Just see that the letters are sent on. And tell Stevens to exhibit all the purple chrysanthemums next Monday and to wire me the result."

A QUESTION OF DIPLOMACY.

The Foreign Minister was down with the gout. For a week he had been confined to the house, and he had missed two Cabinet Councils at a time when the pressure upon his department was severe. It is true that he had an excellent undersecretary and an admirable staff, but the Minister was a man of such ripe experience and of such proven sagacity that things halted in his absence. When his firm hand was at the wheel the great ship of State rode easily and smoothly upon her way; when it was removed she yawed and staggered until twelve British editors rose up in their omniscience and traced out twelve several courses, each of which was the sole and only path to safety. Then it was that the Opposition said vain things, and that the harassed Prime Minister prayed for his absent colleague.

The Foreign Minister sat in his dressing-room in the great house in Cavendish Square. It was May, and the square garden shot up like a veil of green in front of his window, but, in spite of the sunshine, a fire crackled and sputtered in the grate of the sick-room. In a deep-red plush armchair sat the great statesman, his head leaning back upon a silken pillow, one foot stretched forward and supported upon a padded rest. His deeply-lined, finely-chiselled face and slow-moving, heavily-pouched eyes were turned upwards towards the carved and painted ceiling, with that inscrutable expression which had been the despair and the admiration of his Continental colleagues upon the occasion of the famous Congress when he had made his first appearance in the arena of European diplomacy. Yet at the present moment his capacity for hiding his emotions had for the instant failed him, for about the lines of his strong, straight mouth and the puckers of his broad, overhanging forehead, there were sufficient indications of the restlessness and impatience which consumed him.

And indeed there was enough to make a man chafe, for he had much to think of and yet was bereft of the power of thought. There was, for example, that question of the Dobrutscha and the navigation of the mouths of the Danube which was ripe for settlement. The Russian Chancellor had sent a masterly statement upon the subject, and it was the pet ambition of our Minister to answer it in a worthy fashion. Then there was the blockade of Crete, and the British fleet lying off Cape Matapan, waiting for instructions which might change the course of European history. And there were those three unfortunate Macedonian tourists, whose friends were momentarily expecting to receive their ears or their fingers in default of the exorbitant ransom which had been demanded. They must be plucked out of those mountains, by force or by diplomacy, or an outraged public would vent its wrath upon Downing Street. All these questions pressed for a solution, and yet here was the Foreign Minister of England, planted in an arm-chair, with his whole thoughts and attention riveted upon the ball of his right toe! It was humiliating—horribly humiliating! His reason revolted at it. He had been a respecter of himself, a respecter of his own will; but what sort of a machine was it which could be utterly thrown out of gear by a little piece of inflamed gristle? He groaned and writhed among his cushions.

But, after all, was it quite impossible that he should go down to the House? Perhaps the doctor was exaggerating the situation. There was a Cabinet Council that day. He glanced at his watch. It must be nearly over by now. But at least he might perhaps venture to drive down as far as Westminster. He pushed back the little round table with its bristle of medicine-bottles, and levering himself up with a hand upon either arm of the chair, he clutched a thick oak stick and hobbled slowly across the room. For a moment as he moved, his energy of mind and body seemed to return to him. The British fleet should sail from Matapan. Pressure should be brought to bear upon the Turks. The Greeks should be shown—Ow! In an instant the Mediterranean was blotted out, and nothing remained but that huge, undeniable, intrusive, red-hot toe. He staggered to the window and rested his left hand upon the ledge, while he propped himself upon his stick with his right. Outside lay the bright, cool, square garden, a few well-dressed passers-by, and a single, neatly-appointed carriage, which was driving away from his own door. His quick eye caught the coat-of-arms on the panel, and his lips set for a moment and his bushy eyebrows gathered ominously with a deep furrow between them. He hobbled back to his seat and struck the gong which stood upon the table.

"Your mistress!" said he as the serving-man entered.

It was clear that it was impossible to think of going to the House. The shooting up his leg warned him that his doctor had not overestimated the situation. But he had a little mental worry now which had for the moment eclipsed his physical ailments. He tapped the ground impatiently with his stick until the door of the dressing-room swung open, and a tall, elegant lady of rather more than middle age swept into the chamber. Her hair was touched with grey, but her calm, sweet face had all the freshness of youth, and her gown of green shot plush, with a sparkle of gold passementerie at her bosom and shoulders, showed off the lines of her fine figure to their best advantage.

"You sent for me, Charles?"

"Whose carriage was that which drove away just now?"

"Oh, you've been up!" she cried, shaking an admonitory forefinger. "What an old dear it is! How can you be so rash? What am I to say to Sir William when he comes? You know that he gives up his cases when they are insubordinate."

"In this instance the case may give him up," said the Minister, peevishly; "but I must beg, Clara, that you will answer my question."

"Oh! the carriage! It must have been Lord Arthur Sibthorpe's."

"I saw the three chevrons upon the panel," muttered the invalid.

His lady had pulled herself a little straighter and opened her large blue eyes.

"Then why ask?" she said. "One might almost think, Charles, that you were laying a trap! Did you expect that I should deceive you? You have not had your lithia powder."

"For Heaven's sake, leave it alone! I asked because I was surprised that Lord Arthur should call here. I should have fancied, Clara, that I had made myself sufficiently clear on that point. Who received him?"

"I did. That is, I and Ida."

"I will not have him brought into contact with Ida. I do not approve of it. The matter has gone too far already."

Lady Clara seated herself on a velvet-topped footstool, and bent her stately figure over the Minister's hand, which she patted softly between her own.

"Now you have said it, Charles," said she. "It has gone too far—I give you my word, dear, that I never suspected it until it was past all mending. I may be to blame—no doubt I am; but it was all so sudden. The tail end of the season and a week at Lord Donnythorne's. That was all. But oh! Charlie, she loves him so, and she is our only one! How can we make her miserable?"

"Tut, tut!" cried the Minister impatiently, slapping on the plush arm of his chair. "This is too much. I tell you, Clara, I give you my word, that all my official duties, all the affairs of this great empire, do not give me the trouble that Ida does."

"But she is our only one, Charles."

"The more reason that she should not make a mesalliance."

"Mesalliance, Charles! Lord Arthur Sibthorpe, son of the Duke of Tavistock, with a pedigree from the Heptarchy. Debrett takes them right back to Morcar, Earl of Northumberland."

The Minister shrugged his shoulders.

"Lord Arthur is the fourth son of the poorest duke in England," said he. "He has neither prospects nor profession."

"But, oh! Charlie, you could find him both."

"I do not like him. I do not care for the connection."

"But consider Ida! You know how frail her health is. Her whole soul is set upon him. You would not have the heart, Charles, to separate them?"

There was a tap at the door. Lady Clara swept towards it and threw it open.

"Yes, Thomas?"

"If you please, my lady, the Prime Minister is below."

"Show him up, Thomas."

"Now, Charlie, you must not excite yourself over public matters. Be very good and cool and reasonable, like a darling. I am sure that I may trust you."

She threw her light shawl round the invalid's shoulders, and slipped away into the bed-room as the great man was ushered in at the door of the dressing-room.

"My dear Charles," said he cordially, stepping into the room with all the boyish briskness for which he was famous, "I trust that you find yourself a little better. Almost ready for harness, eh? We miss you sadly, both in the House and in the Council. Quite a storm brewing over this Grecian business. The Times took a nasty line this morning."

"So I saw," said the invalid, smiling up at his chief. "Well, well, we must let them see that the country is not entirely ruled from Printing House Square yet. We must keep our own course without faltering."

"Certainly, Charles, most undoubtedly," assented the Prime Minister, with his hands in his pockets.

"It was so kind of you to call. I am all impatience to know what was done in the Council."

"Pure formalities, nothing more. By-the-way, the Macedonian prisoners are all right."

"Thank Goodness for that!"

"We adjourned all other business until we should have you with us next week. The question of a dissolution begins to press. The reports from the provinces are excellent."

The Foreign Minister moved impatiently and groaned.

"We must really straighten up our foreign business a little," said he. "I must get Novikoff's Note answered. It is clever, but the fallacies are obvious. I wish, too, we could clear up the Afghan frontier. This illness is most exasperating. There is so much to be done, but my brain is clouded. Sometimes I think it is the gout, and sometimes I put it down to the colchicum."

"What will our medical autocrat say?" laughed the Prime Minister. "You are so irreverent, Charles. With a bishop one may feel at one's ease. They are not beyond the reach of argument. But a doctor with his stethoscope and thermometer is a thing apart. Your reading does not impinge upon him. He is serenely above you. And then, of course, he takes you at a disadvantage. With health and strength one might cope with him. Have you read Hahnemann? What are your views upon Hahnemann?"

The invalid knew his illustrious colleague too well to follow him down any of those by-paths of knowledge in which he delighted to wander. To his intensely shrewd and practical mind there was something repellent in the waste of energy involved in a discussion upon the Early Church or the twenty-seven principles of Mesmer. It was his custom to slip past such conversational openings with a quick step and an averted face.

"I have hardly glanced at his writings," said he. "By-the-way, I suppose that there was no special departmental news?"

"Ah! I had almost forgotten. Yes, it was one of the things which I had called to tell you. Sir Algernon Jones has resigned at Tangier. There is a vacancy there."

"It had better be filled at once. The longer delay the more applicants."

"Ah, patronage, patronage!" sighed the Prime Minister. "Every vacancy makes one doubtful friend and a dozen very positive enemies. Who so bitter as the disappointed place-seeker? But you are right, Charles. Better fill it at once, especially as there is some little trouble in Morocco. I understand that the Duke of Tavistock would like the place for his fourth son, Lord Arthur Sibthorpe. We are under some obligation to the Duke."

The Foreign Minister sat up eagerly.

"My dear friend," he said, "it is the very appointment which I should have suggested. Lord Arthur would be very much better in Tangier at present than in—in——"

"Cavendish Square?" hazarded his chief, with a little arch query of his eyebrows.

"Well, let us say London. He has manner and tact. He was at Constantinople in Norton's time."

"Then he talks Arabic?"

"A smattering. But his French is good."

"Speaking of Arabic, Charles, have you dipped into Averroes?"

"No, I have not. But the appointment would be an excellent one in every way. Would you have the great goodness to arrange the matter in my absence?"

"Certainly, Charles, certainly. Is there anything else that I can do?"

"No. I hope to be in the House by Monday."

"I trust so. We miss you at every turn. The Times will try to make mischief over that Grecian business. A leader-writer is a terribly irresponsible thing, Charles. There is no method by which he may be confuted, however preposterous his assertions. Good-bye! Read Porson! Goodbye!"

He shook the invalid's hand, gave a jaunty wave of his broad-brimmed hat, and darted out of the room with the same elasticity and energy with which he had entered it.

The footman had already opened the great folding door to usher the illustrious visitor to his carriage, when a lady stepped from the drawing-room and touched him on the sleeve. From behind the half-closed portière of stamped velvet a little pale face peeped out, half-curious, half-frightened.

"May I have one word?"

"Surely, Lady Clara."

"I hope it is not intrusive. I would not for the world overstep the limits——"

"My dear Lady Clara!" interrupted the Prime Minister, with a youthful bow and wave.

"Pray do not answer me if I go too far. But I know that Lord Arthur Sibthorpe has applied for Tangier. Would it be a liberty if I asked you what chance he has?"

"The post is filled up."

"Oh!"

In the foreground and background there was a disappointed face.

"And Lord Arthur has it."

The Prime Minister chuckled over his little piece of roguery.

"We have just decided it," he continued.

"Lord Arthur must go in a week. I am delighted to perceive, Lady Clara, that the appointment has your approval. Tangier is a place of extraordinary interest. Catherine of Braganza and Colonel Kirke will occur to your memory. Burton has written well upon Northern Africa. I dine at Windsor, so I am sure that you will excuse my leaving you. I trust that Lord Charles will be better. He can hardly fail to be so with such a nurse."

He bowed, waved, and was off down the steps to his brougham. As he drove away, Lady Clara could see that he was already deeply absorbed in a paper-covered novel.

She pushed back the velvet curtains, and returned into the drawing-room. Her daughter stood in the sunlight by the window, tall, fragile, and exquisite, her features and outline not unlike her mother's, but frailer, softer, more delicate. The golden light struck one half of her high-bred, sensitive face, and glimmered upon her thickly-coiled flaxen hair, striking a pinkish tint from her closely-cut costume of fawn-coloured cloth with its dainty cinnamon ruchings. One little soft frill of chiffon nestled round her throat, from which the white, graceful neck and well-poised head shot up like a lily amid moss. Her thin white hands were pressed together, and her blue eyes turned beseechingly upon her mother.

"Silly girl! Silly girl!" said the matron, answering that imploring look. She put her hands upon her daughter's sloping shoulders and drew her towards her. "It is a very nice place for a short time. It will be a stepping stone."

"But oh! mamma, in a week! Poor Arthur!"

"He will be happy."

"What! happy to part?"

"He need not part. You shall go with him."

"Oh! mamma!"

"Yes, I say it."

"Oh! mamma, in a week?"

"Yes indeed. A great deal may be done in a week. I shall order your trousseau to-day."

"Oh! you dear, sweet angel! But I am so frightened! And papa? Oh! dear, I am so frightened!"

"Your papa is a diplomatist, dear."

"Yes, ma."

"But, between ourselves, he married a diplomatist too. If he can manage the British Empire, I think that I can manage him, Ida. How long have you been engaged, child?"

"Ten weeks, mamma."

"Then it is quite time it came to a head. Lord Arthur cannot leave England without you. You must go to Tangier as the Minister's wife. Now, you will sit there on the settee, dear, and let me manage entirely. There is Sir William's carriage! I do think that I know how to manage Sir William. James, just ask the doctor to step in this way!"

A heavy, two-horsed carriage had drawn up at the door, and there came a single stately thud upon the knocker. An instant afterwards the drawing-room door flew open and the footman ushered in the famous physician. He was a small man, clean-shaven, with the old-fashioned black dress and white cravat with high-standing collar. He swung his golden pince-nez in his right hand as he walked, and bent forward with a peering, blinking expression, which was somehow suggestive of the dark and complex cases through which he had seen.

"Ah," said he, as he entered. "My young patient! I am glad of the opportunity."

"Yes, I wish to speak to you about her, Sir William. Pray take this arm-chair."

"Thank you, I will sit beside her," said he, taking his place upon the settee. "She is looking better, less anaemic unquestionably, and a fuller pulse. Quite a little tinge of colour, and yet not hectic."

"I feel stronger, Sir William."

"But she still has the pain in the side."

"Ah, that pain!" He tapped lightly under the collar-bones, and then bent forward with his biaural stethoscope in either ear. "Still a trace of dulness— still a slight crepitation," he murmured.

"You spoke of a change, doctor."

"Yes, certainly a judicious change might be advisable."

"You said a dry climate. I wish to do to the letter what you recommend."

"You have always been model patients."

"We wish to be. You said a dry climate."

"Did I? I rather forget the particulars of our conversation. But a dry climate is certainly indicated."

"Which one?"

"Well, I think really that a patient should be allowed some latitude. I must not exact too rigid discipline. There is room for individual choice—the Engadine, Central Europe, Egypt, Algiers, which you like."

"I hear that Tangier is also recommended."

"Oh, yes, certainly; it is very dry."

"You hear, Ida? Sir William says that you are to go to Tangier."

"Or any——"

"No, no, Sir William! We feel safest when we are most obedient. You have said Tangier, and we shall certainly try Tangier."

"Really, Lady Clara, your implicit faith is most flattering. It is not everyone who would sacrifice their own plans and inclinations so readily."

"We know your skill and your experience, Sir William. Ida shall try Tangier. I am convinced that she will be benefited."

"I have no doubt of it."

"But you know Lord Charles. He is just a little inclined to decide medical matters as he would an affair of State. I hope that you will be firm with him."

"As long as Lord Charles honours me so far as to ask my advice I am sure that he would not place me in the false position of having that advice disregarded."

The medical baronet whirled round the cord of his pince-nez and pushed out a protesting hand.

"No, no, but you must be firm on the point of Tangier."

"Having deliberately formed the opinion that Tangier is the best place for our young patient, I do not think that I shall readily change my conviction."

"Of course not."

"I shall speak to Lord Charles upon the subject now when I go upstairs."

"Pray do."

"And meanwhile she will continue her present course of treatment. I trust that the warm African air may send her back in a few months with all her energy restored."

He bowed in the courteous, sweeping, old-world fashion which had done so much to build up his ten thousand a year, and, with the stealthy gait of a man whose life is spent in sick-rooms, he followed the footman upstairs.

As the red velvet curtains swept back into position, the Lady Ida threw her arms round her mother's neck and sank her face on to her bosom.

"Oh! mamma, you ARE a diplomatist!" she cried.

But her mother's expression was rather that of the general who looked upon the first smoke of the guns than of one who had won the victory.

"All will be right, dear," said she, glancing down at the fluffy yellow curls and tiny ear. "There is still much to be done, but I think we may venture to order the trousseau."

"Oh I how brave you are!"

"Of course, it will in any case be a very quiet affair. Arthur must get the license. I do not approve of hole-and-corner marriages, but where the gentleman has to take up an official position some allowance must be made. We can have Lady Hilda Edgecombe, and the Trevors, and the Grevilles, and I am sure that the Prime Minister would run down if he could."

"And papa?"

"Oh, yes; he will come too, if he is well enough. We must wait until Sir William goes, and, meanwhile, I shall write to Lord Arthur."

Half an hour had passed, and quite a number of notes had been dashed off in the fine, bold, park-paling handwriting of the Lady Clara, when the door clashed, and the wheels of the doctor's carriage were heard grating outside against the kerb. The Lady Clara laid down her pen, kissed her daughter, and started off for the sick-room. The Foreign Minister was lying back in his chair, with a red silk handkerchief over his forehead, and his bulbous, cotton-wadded foot still protruding upon its rest.

"I think it is almost liniment time," said Lady Clara, shaking a blue crinkled bottle. "Shall I put on a little?"

"Oh! this pestilent toe!" groaned the sufferer. "Sir William won't hear of my moving yet. I do think he is the most completely obstinate and pig-headed man that I have ever met. I tell him that he has mistaken his profession, and that I could find him a post at Constantinople. We need a mule out there."

"Poor Sir William!" laughed Lady Clara. "But how has he roused your wrath?"

"He is so persistent-so dogmatic."

"Upon what point?"

"Well, he has been laying down the law about Ida. He has decreed, it seems, that she is to go to Tangier."

"He said something to that effect before he went up to you."

"Oh, he did, did he?"

The slow-moving, inscrutable eye came sliding round to her.

Lady Clara's face had assumed an expression of transparent obvious innocence, an intrusive candour which is never seen in nature save when a woman is bent upon deception.

"He examined her lungs, Charles. He did not say much, but his expression was very grave."

"Not to say owlish," interrupted the Minister.

"No, no, Charles; it is no laughing matter. He said that she must have a change. I am sure that he thought more than he said. He spoke of dulness and crepitation, and the effects of the African air. Then the talk turned upon dry, bracing health resorts, and he agreed that Tangier was the place. He said that even a few months there would work a change."

"And that was all?"

"Yes, that was all."

Lord Charles shrugged his shoulders with the air of a man who is but half convinced.

"But of course," said Lady Clara, serenely, "if you think it better that Ida should not go she shall not. The only thing is that if she should get worse we might feel a little uncomfortable afterwards. In a weakness of that sort a very short time may make a difference. Sir William evidently thought the matter critical. Still, there is no reason why he should influence you. It is a little responsibility, however. If you take it all upon yourself and free me from any of it, so that afterwards———"

"My dear Clara, how you do croak!"

"Oh! I don't wish to do that, Charles. But you remember what happened to Lord Bellamy's child. She was just Ida's age. That was another case in which Sir William's advice was disregarded."

Lord Charles groaned impatiently.

"I have not disregarded it," said he.

"No, no, of course not. I know your strong sense, and your good heart too well, dear. You were very wisely looking at both sides of the question. That is what we poor women cannot do. It is emotion against reason, as I have often heard you say. We are swayed this way and that, but you men are persistent, and so you gain your way with us. But I am so pleased that you have decided for Tangier."

"Have I?"

"Well, dear, you said that you would not disregard Sir William."

"Well, Clara, admitting that Ida is to go to Tangier, you will allow that it is impossible for me to escort her?"

"Utterly."

"And for you?"

"While you are ill my place is by your side."

"There is your sister?"

"She is going to Florida."

"Lady Dumbarton, then?"

"She is nursing her father. It is out of the question."

"Well, then, whom can we possibly ask? Especially just as the season is commencing. You see, Clara, the fates fight against Sir William."

His wife rested her elbows against the back of the great red chair, and passed her fingers through the statesman's grizzled curls, stooping down as she did so until her lips were close to his ear.

"There is Lord Arthur Sibthorpe," said she softly.

Lord Charles bounded in his chair, and muttered a word or two such as were more frequently heard from Cabinet Ministers in Lord Melbourne's time than now.

"Are you mad, Clara!" he cried. "What can have put such a thought into your head?"

"The Prime Minister."

"Who? The Prime Minister?"

"Yes, dear. Now do, do be good! Or perhaps I had better not speak to you about it any more."

"Well, I really think that you have gone rather too far to retreat."

"It was the Prime Minister, then, who told me that Lord Arthur was going to Tangier."

"It is a fact, though it had escaped my memory for the instant."

"And then came Sir William with his advice about Ida. Oh! Charlie, it is surely more than a coincidence!"

"I am convinced," said Lord Charles, with his shrewd, questioning gaze, "that it is very much more than a coincidence, Lady Clara. You are a very clever woman, my dear. A born manager and organiser."

Lady Clara brushed past the compliment.

"Think of our own young days, Charlie," she whispered, with her fingers still toying with his hair. "What were you then? A poor man, not even Ambassador at Tangier. But I loved you, and believed in you, and have I ever regretted it? Ida loves and believes in Lord Arthur, and why should she ever regret it either?"

Lord Charles was silent. His eyes were fixed upon the green branches which waved outside the window; but his mind had flashed back to a Devonshire country-house of thirty years ago, and to the one fateful evening when, between old yew hedges, he paced along beside a slender girl, and poured out to her his hopes, his fears, and his ambitious. He took the white, thin hand and pressed it to his lips.

"You, have been a good wife to me, Clara," said he.

She said nothing. She did not attempt to improve upon her advantage. A less consummate general might have tried to do so, and ruined all. She stood silent and submissive, noting the quick play of thought which peeped from his eyes and lip. There was a sparkle in the one and a twitch of amusement in the other, as he at last glanced up at her.

"Clara," said he, "deny it if you can! You have ordered the trousseau."

She gave his ear a little pinch.

"Subject to your approval," said she.

"You have written to the Archbishop."

"It is not posted yet."

"You have sent a note to Lord Arthur."

"How could you tell that?"

"He is downstairs now."

"No; but I think that is his brougham."

Lord Charles sank back with a look of half-comical despair.

"Who is to fight against such a woman?" he cried. "Oh! if I could send you to Novikoff! He is too much for any of my men. But, Clara, I cannot have them up here."

"Not for your blessing?"

"No, no!"

"It would make them so happy."

"I cannot stand scenes."

"Then I shall convey it to them."

"And pray say no more about it—to-day, at any rate. I have been weak over the matter."

"Oh! Charlie, you who are so strong!"

"You have outflanked me, Clara. It was very well done. I must congratulate you."

"Well," she murmured, as she kissed him, "you know I have been studying a very clever diplomatist for thirty years."

A MEDICAL DOCUMENT.

Medical men are, as a class, very much too busy to take stock of singular situations or dramatic events. Thus it happens that the ablest chronicler of their experiences in our literature was a lawyer. A life spent in watching over death-beds—or over birth-beds which are infinitely more trying—takes something from a man's sense of proportion, as constant strong waters might corrupt his palate. The overstimulated nerve ceases to respond. Ask the surgeon for his best experiences and he may reply that he has seen little that is remarkable, or break away into the technical. But catch him some night when the fire has spurted up and his pipe is reeking, with a few of his brother practitioners for company and an artful question or allusion to set him going. Then you will get some raw, green facts new plucked from the tree of life.

It is after one of the quarterly dinners of the Midland Branch of the British

Medical Association. Twenty coffee cups, a dozer liqueur glasses, and a solid bank of blue smoke which swirls slowly along the high, gilded ceiling gives a hint of a successful gathering. But the members have shredded off to their homes. The line of heavy, bulge-pocketed overcoats and of stethoscope-bearing top hats is gone from the hotel corridor. Round the fire in the sitting-room three medicos are still lingering, however, all smoking and arguing, while a fourth, who is a mere layman and young at that, sits back at the table. Under cover of an open journal he is writing furiously with a stylographic pen, asking a question in an innocent voice from time to time and so flickering up the conversation whenever it shows a tendency to wane.

The three men are all of that staid middle age which begins early and lasts late in the profession. They are none of them famous, yet each is of good repute, and a fair type of his particular branch. The portly man with the authoritative manner and the white, vitriol splash upon his cheek is Charley Manson, chief of the Wormley Asylum, and author of the brilliant monograph—Obscure Nervous Lesions in the Unmarried. He always wears his collar high like that, since the half-successful attempt of a student of Revelations to cut his throat with a splinter of glass. The second, with the ruddy face and the merry brown eyes, is a general practitioner, a man of vast experience, who, with his three assistants and his five horses, takes twenty-five hundred a year in half-crown visits and shilling consultations out of the poorest quarter of a great city. That cheery face of Theodore Foster is seen at the side of a hundred sick-beds a day, and if he has one-third more names on his visiting list than in his cash book he always promises himself that he will get level some day when a millionaire with a chronic complaint—the ideal combination—shall seek his services. The third, sitting on the right with his dress shoes shining on the top of the fender, is Hargrave, the rising surgeon. His face has none of the broad humanity of Theodore Foster's, the eye is stern and critical, the mouth straight and severe, but there is strength and decision in every line of it, and it is nerve rather than sympathy which the patient demands when he is bad enough to come to Hargrave's door. He calls himself a jawman "a mere jawman" as he modestly puts it, but in point of fact he is too young and too poor to confine himself to a specialty, and there is nothing surgical which Hargrave has not the skill and the audacity to do.

"Before, after, and during," murmurs the general practitioner in answer to some interpolation of the outsider's. "I assure you, Manson, one sees all sorts of evanescent forms of madness."

"Ah, puerperal!" throws in the other, knocking the curved grey ash from his cigar. "But you had some case in your mind, Foster."

"Well, there was only one last week which was new to me. I had been engaged by some people of the name of Silcoe. When the trouble came round I went myself, for they would not hear of an assistant. The husband who was a policeman, was sitting at the head of the bed on the further side. 'This won't do,' said I. 'Oh yes, doctor, it must do,' said she. 'It's quite irregular and he must go,' said I. 'It's that or nothing,' said she. 'I won't open my mouth or stir a finger the whole night,' said he. So it ended by my allowing him to remain, and there he sat for eight hours on end. She was very good over the matter, but every now and again HE would fetch a hollow groan, and I noticed that he held his right hand just under the sheet all the time, where I had no doubt that it was clasped by her left. When it was all happily over, I looked at him and his face was the colour of this cigar ash, and his head had dropped on to the edge of the pillow. Of course I thought he had fainted with emotion, and I was just telling myself what I thought of myself for having been such a fool as to let him stay there, when suddenly I saw that the sheet over his hand was all soaked with blood; I whisked it down, and there was the fellow's wrist half cut through. The woman had one bracelet of a policeman's handcuff over her left wrist and the other round his right one. When she had been in pain she had twisted with all her strength and the iron had fairly eaten into the bone of the man's arm. 'Aye, doctor,' said she, when she saw I had noticed it. 'He's got to take his share as well as me. Turn and turn,' said she."

"Don't you find it a very wearing branch of the profession?" asks Foster after a pause.

"My dear fellow, it was the fear of it that drove me into lunacy work."

"Aye, and it has driven men into asylums who never found their way on to the medical staff. I was a very shy fellow myself as a student, and I know what it means."

"No joke that in general practice," says the alienist.

"Well, you hear men talk about it as though it were, but I tell you it's much nearer tragedy. Take some poor, raw, young fellow who has just put up his plate in a strange town. He has found it a trial all his life, perhaps, to talk to a woman about lawn tennis and church services. When a young man IS shy he is shyer than any girl. Then down comes an anxious mother and consults him upon the most intimate family matters. 'I shall never go to that doctor again,' says she afterwards. 'His manner is so stiff and unsympathetic.' Unsympathetic! Why, the poor lad was struck dumb and paralysed. I have known general practitioners who were so shy that they could not bring themselves to ask the way in the street. Fancy what sensitive men like that must endure before they get broken in to medical practice. And then they know that nothing is so catching as shyness, and that if they do not keep a face of stone, their patient will be covered with confusion. And so they keep their face of stone, and earn the reputation perhaps of having a heart to correspond. I suppose nothing would shake YOUR nerve, Manson."

"Well, when a man lives year in year out among a thousand lunatics, with a fair sprinkling of homicidals among them, one's nerves either get set or shattered. Mine are all right so far."

"I was frightened once," says the surgeon. "It was when I was doing dispensary work. One night I had a call from some very poor people, and gathered from the few words they said that their child was ill. When I entered the room I saw a small cradle in the corner. Raising the lamp I walked over and putting back the curtains I looked down at the baby. I tell you it was sheer Providence that I didn't drop that lamp and set the whole place alight. The head on the pillow turned and I saw a face looking up at me which seemed to me to have more malignancy and wickedness than ever I had dreamed of in a nightmare. It was the flush of red over the cheekbones, and the brooding eyes full of loathing of me, and of everything else, that impressed me. I'll never forget my start as, instead of the chubby face of an infant, my eyes fell upon this creature. I took the mother into the next room. 'What is it?' I asked. 'A girl of sixteen,' said she, and then throwing up her arms, 'Oh, pray God she may be taken!' The poor thing, though she spent her life in this little cradle, had great, long, thin limbs which she curled up under her. I lost sight of the case and don't know what became of it, but I'll never forget the look in her eyes."

"That's creepy," says Dr. Foster. "But I think one of my experiences would run it close. Shortly after I put up my plate I had a visit from a little hunch-backed woman who wished me to come and attend to her sister in her trouble. When I reached the house, which was a very poor one, I found two other little hunched-backed women, exactly like the first, waiting for me in the sitting-room. Not one of them said a word, but my companion took the lamp and walked upstairs with her two sisters behind her, and me bringing up the rear. I can see those three queer shadows cast by the lamp upon the wall as clearly as I can see that tobacco pouch. In the room above was the fourth sister, a remarkably beautiful girl in evident need of my assistance. There was no wedding ring upon her finger. The three deformed sisters seated themselves round the room, like so many graven images, and all night not one of them opened her mouth. I'm not romancing, Hargrave; this is absolute fact. In the early morning a fearful thunderstorm broke out, one of the most violent I have ever known. The little garret burned blue with the lightning, and thunder roared and rattled as if it were on the very roof of the house. It wasn't much of a lamp I had, and it was a queer thing when a spurt of lightning came to see those three twisted figures sitting round the walls, or to have the voice of my patient drowned by the booming of the thunder. By Jove! I don't mind telling you that there was a time when I nearly bolted from the room. All came right in the end, but I never heard the true story of the unfortunate beauty and her three crippled sisters."

"That's the worst of these medical stories," sighs the outsider. "They never seem to have an end."

"When a man is up to his neck in practice, my boy, he has no time to gratify his private curiosity. Things shoot across him and he gets a glimpse of them, only to recall them, perhaps, at some quiet moment like this. But I've always felt, Manson, that your line had as much of the terrible in it as any other."

"More," groans the alienist. "A disease of the body is bad enough, but this seems to be a disease of the soul. Is it not a shocking thing—a thing to drive a reasoning man into absolute Materialism—to think that you may have a fine, noble fellow with every divine instinct and that some little vascular change, the dropping, we will say, of a minute spicule of bone from the inner table of his skull on to the surface of his brain may have the effect of changing him to a filthy and pitiable creature with every low and debasing tendency? What a satire an asylum is upon the majesty of man, and no less upon the ethereal nature of the soul."

"Faith and hope," murmurs the general practitioner.

"I have no faith, not much hope, and all the charity I can afford," says the surgeon. "When theology squares itself with the facts of life I'll read it up."

"You were talking about cases," says the outsider, jerking the ink down into his stylographic pen.

"Well, take a common complaint which kills many thousands every year, like G. P. for instance."

"What's G. P.?"

"General practitioner," suggests the surgeon with a grin.

"The British public will have to know what G. P. is," says the alienist gravely. "It's increasing by leaps and bounds, and it has the distinction of being absolutely incurable. General paralysis is its full title, and I tell you it promises to be a perfect scourge. Here's a fairly typical case now which I saw last Monday week. A young farmer, a splendid fellow, surprised his fellows by taking a very rosy view of things at a time when the whole country-side was grumbling. He was going to give up wheat, give up arable land, too, if it didn't pay, plant two thousand acres of rhododendrons and get a monopoly of the supply for Covent Garden—there was no end to his schemes, all sane enough but just a bit inflated. I called at the farm, not to see him, but on an altogether different matter. Something about the man's way of talking struck me and I watched him narrowly. His lip had a trick of quivering, his words slurred themselves together, and so did his handwriting when he had occasion to draw up a small agreement. A closer inspection showed me that one of his pupils was ever so little larger than the other. As I left the house his wife came after me. 'Isn't it splendid to see Job looking so well, doctor,' said she; 'he's that full of energy he can hardly keep himself quiet.' I did not say anything, for I had not the heart, but I knew that the fellow was as much condemned to death as though he were lying in the cell at Newgate. It was a characteristic case of incipient G. P."

"Good heavens!" cries the outsider. "My own lips tremble. I often slur my words. I believe I've got it myself."

Three little chuckles come from the front of the fire.

"There's the danger of a little medical knowledge to the layman."

"A great authority has said that every first year's student is suffering in silent agony from four diseases," remarks the surgeon. "One is heart disease, of course; another is cancer of the parotid. I forget the two other."

"Where does the parotid come in?"

"Oh, it's the last wisdom tooth coming through!"

"And what would be the end of that young farmer?" asks the outsider.

"Paresis of all the muscles, ending in fits, coma, and death. It may be a few months, it may be a year or two. He was a very strong young man and would take some killing."

"By-the-way," says the alienist, "did I ever tell you about the first certificate I signed? I came as near ruin then as a man could go."

"What was it, then?"

"I was in practice at the time. One morning a Mrs. Cooper called upon me and informed me that her husband had shown signs of delusions lately. They took the form of imagining that he had been in the army and had distinguished himself very much. As a matter of fact he was a lawyer and had never been out of England. Mrs. Cooper was of opinion that if I were to call it might alarm him, so it was agreed between us that she should send him up in the evening on some pretext to my consulting-room, which would give me the opportunity of having a chat with him and, if I were convinced of his insanity, of signing his certificate. Another doctor had already signed, so that it only needed my concurrence to have him placed under treatment. Well, Mr. Cooper arrived in the evening about half an hour before I had expected him, and consulted me as to some malarious symptoms from which he said that he suffered. According to his account he had just returned from the Abyssinian Campaign, and had been one of the first of the British forces to enter Magdala. No delusion could possibly be more marked, for he would talk of little else, so I filled in the papers without the slightest hesitation. When his wife arrived, after he had left, I put some questions to her to complete the form. 'What is his age?' I asked. 'Fifty,' said she. 'Fifty!' I cried. 'Why, the man I examined could not have been more than thirty! And so it came out that the real Mr. Cooper had never called upon me at all, but that by one of those coincidences which take a man's breath away another Cooper, who really was a very distinguished young officer of artillery, had come in to consult me. My pen was wet to sign the paper when I discovered it," says Dr. Manson, mopping his forehead.

"We were talking about nerve just now," observes the surgeon. "Just after my qualifying I served in the Navy for a time, as I think you know. I was on the flag-ship on the West African Station, and I remember a singular example of nerve which came to my notice at that time. One of our small gunboats had gone up the Calabar river, and while there the surgeon died of coast fever. On the same day a man's leg was broken by a spar falling upon it, and it became quite obvious that it must be taken off above the knee if his life was to be saved. The young lieutenant who was in charge of the craft searched among the dead doctor's effects and laid his hands upon some chloroform, a hip-joint knife, and a volume of Grey's Anatomy. He had the man laid by the steward upon the cabin table, and with a picture of a cross section of the thigh in front of him he began to take off the limb. Every now and then, referring to the diagram, he would say: 'Stand by with the lashings, steward. There's blood on the chart about here.' Then he would jab with his knife until he cut the artery, and he and his assistant would tie it up before they went any further. In this way they gradually whittled the leg off, and upon my word they made a very excellent job of it. The man is hopping about the Portsmouth Hard at this day.

"It's no joke when the doctor of one of these isolated gunboats himself falls ill," continues the surgeon after a pause. "You might think it easy for him to prescribe for himself, but this fever knocks you down like a club, and you haven't strength left to brush a mosquito off your face. I had a touch of it at Lagos, and I know what I am telling you. But there was a chum of mine who really had a curious experience. The whole crew gave him up, and, as they had never had a funeral aboard the ship, they began rehearsing the forms so as to be ready. They thought that he was unconscious, but he swears he could hear every word that passed. 'Corpse comin' up the latchway!' cried the Cockney sergeant of Marines. 'Present harms!' He was so amused, and so indignant too, that he just made up his mind that he wouldn't be carried through that hatchway, and he wasn't, either."

"There's no need for fiction in medicine," remarks Foster, "for the facts will always beat anything you can fancy. But it has seemed to me sometimes that a curious paper might be read at some of these meetings about the uses of medicine in popular fiction."

"How?"

"Well, of what the folk die of, and what diseases are made most use of in novels. Some are worn to pieces, and others, which are equally common in real life, are never mentioned. Typhoid is fairly frequent, but scarlet fever is unknown. Heart disease is common, but then heart disease, as we know it, is usually the sequel of some foregoing disease, of which we never hear anything in the romance. Then there is the mysterious malady called brain fever, which always attacks the heroine after a crisis, but which is unknown under that name to the text books. People when they are over-excited in novels fall down in a fit. In a fairly large experience I have never known anyone do so in real life. The small complaints simply don't exist. Nobody ever gets shingles or quinsy, or mumps in a novel. All the diseases, too, belong to the upper part of the body. The novelist never strikes below the belt."

"I'll tell you what, Foster," says the alienist, "there is a side of life which is too medical for the general public and too romantic for the professional journals, but which contains some of the richest human materials that a man could study. It's not a pleasant side, I am afraid, but if it is good enough for Providence to create, it is good enough for us to try and understand. It would deal with strange outbursts of savagery and vice in the lives of the best men, curious momentary weaknesses in the record of the sweetest women, known but to one or two, and inconceivable to the world around. It would deal, too, with the singular phenomena of waxing and of waning manhood, and would throw a light upon those actions which have cut short many an honoured career and sent a man to a prison when he should have been hurried to a consulting-room. Of all evils that may come upon the sons of men, God shield us principally from that one!"

"I had a case some little time ago which was out of the ordinary," says the surgeon. "There's a famous beauty in London society—I mention no names—who used to be remarkable a few seasons ago for the very low dresses which she would wear. She had the whitest of skins and most beautiful of shoulders, so it was no wonder. Then gradually the frilling at her neck lapped upwards and upwards, until last year she astonished everyone by wearing quite a high collar at a time when it was completely out of fashion. Well, one day this very woman was shown into my consulting-room. When the footman was gone she suddenly tore off the upper part of her dress. 'For Gods sake do something for me!' she cried. Then I saw what the trouble was. A rodent ulcer was eating its way upwards, coiling on in its serpiginous fashion until the end of it was flush with her collar. The red streak of its trail was lost below the line of her bust. Year by year it had ascended and she had heightened her dress to hide it, until now it was about to invade her face. She had been too proud to confess her trouble, even to a medical man."

"And did you stop it?"

"Well, with zinc chloride I did what I could. But it may break out again. She was one of those beautiful white-and-pink creatures who are rotten with struma. You may patch but you can't mend."

"Dear! dear! dear!" cries the general practitioner, with that kindly softening of the eyes which had endeared him to so many thousands. "I suppose we mustn't think ourselves wiser than Providence, but there are times when one feels that something is wrong in the scheme of things. I've seen some sad things in my life. Did I ever tell you that case where Nature divorced a most loving couple? He was a fine young fellow, an athlete and a gentleman, but he overdid athletics. You know how the force that controls us gives us a little tweak to remind us when we get off the beaten track. It may be a pinch on the great toe if we drink too much and work too little. Or it may be a tug on our nerves if we dissipate energy too much. With the athlete, of course, it's the heart or the lungs. He had bad phthisis and was sent to Davos. Well, as luck would have it, she developed rheumatic fever, which left her heart very much affected. Now, do you see the dreadful dilemma in which those poor people found themselves? When he came below four thousand feet or so, his symptoms became terrible. She could come up about twenty-five hundred and then her heart reached its limit. They had several interviews half way down the valley, which left them nearly dead, and at last, the doctors had to absolutely forbid it. And so for four years they lived within three miles of each other and never met. Every morning he would go to a place which overlooked the chalet in which she lived and would wave a great white cloth and she answer from below. They could see each other quite plainly with their field glasses, and they might have been in different planets for all their chance of meeting."

"And one at last died," says the outsider.

"No, sir. I'm sorry not to be able to clinch the story, but the man recovered and is now a successful stockbroker in Drapers Gardens. The woman, too, is the mother of a considerable family. But what are you doing there?"

"Only taking a note or two of your talk."

The three medical men laugh as they walk towards their overcoats.

"Why, we've done nothing but talk shop," says the general practitioner. "What possible interest can the public take in that?"

LOT NO. 249.

Of the dealings of Edward Bellingham with William Monkhouse Lee, and of the cause of the great terror of Abercrombie Smith, it may be that no absolute and final judgment will ever be delivered. It is true that we have the full and clear narrative of Smith himself, and such corroboration as he could look for from Thomas Styles the servant, from the Reverend Plumptree Peterson, Fellow of Old's, and from such other people as chanced to gain some passing glance at this or that incident in a singular chain of events. Yet, in the main, the story must rest upon Smith alone, and the most will think that it is more likely that one brain, however outwardly sane, has some subtle warp in its texture, some strange flaw in its workings, than that the path of Nature has been overstepped in open day in so famed a centre of learning and light as the University of Oxford. Yet when we think how narrow and how devious this path of Nature is, how dimly we can trace it, for all our lamps of science, and how from the darkness which girds it round great and terrible possibilities loom ever shadowly upwards, it is a bold and confident man who will put a limit to the strange by-paths into which the human spirit may wander.

In a certain wing of what we will call Old College in Oxford there is a corner turret of an exceeding great age. The heavy arch which spans the open door has bent downwards in the centre under the weight of its years, and the grey, lichen-blotched blocks of stone are, bound and knitted together with withes and strands of ivy, as though the old mother had set herself to brace them up against wind and weather. From the door a stone stair curves upward spirally, passing two landings, and terminating in a third one, its steps all shapeless and hollowed by the tread of so many generations of the seekers after knowledge. Life has flowed like water down this winding stair, and, waterlike, has left these smooth-worn grooves behind it. From the long-gowned, pedantic scholars of Plantagenet days down to the young bloods of a later age, how full and strong had been that tide of young English life. And what was left now of all those hopes, those strivings, those fiery energies, save here and there in some old-world churchyard a few scratches upon a stone, and perchance a handful of dust in a mouldering coffin? Yet here were the silent stair and the grey old wall, with bend and saltire and many another heraldic device still to be read upon its surface, like grotesque shadows thrown back from the days that had passed.

In the month of May, in the year 1884, three young men occupied the sets of rooms which opened on to the separate landings of the old stair. Each set consisted simply of a sitting-room and of a bedroom, while the two corresponding rooms upon the ground-floor were used, the one as a coal-cellar, and the other as the living-room of the servant, or gyp, Thomas Styles, whose duty it was to wait upon the three men above him. To right and to left was a line of lecture-rooms and of offices, so that the dwellers in the old turret enjoyed a certain seclusion, which made the chambers popular among the more studious undergraduates. Such were the three who occupied them now— Abercrombie Smith above, Edward Bellingham beneath him, and William Monkhouse Lee upon the lowest storey.

It was ten o'clock on a bright spring night, and Abercrombie Smith lay back in his arm-chair, his feet upon the fender, and his briar-root pipe between his lips. In a similar chair, and equally at his ease, there lounged on the other side of the fireplace his old school friend Jephro Hastie. Both men were in flannels, for they had spent their evening upon the river, but apart from their dress no one could look at their hard-cut, alert faces without seeing that they were open-air men—men whose minds and tastes turned naturally to all that was manly and robust. Hastie, indeed, was stroke of his college boat, and Smith was an even better oar, but a coming examination had already cast its shadow over him and held him to his work, save for the few hours a week which health demanded. A litter of medical books upon the table, with scattered bones, models and anatomical plates, pointed to the extent as well as the nature of his studies, while a couple of single-sticks and a set of boxing-gloves above the mantelpiece hinted at the means by which, with Hastie's help, he might take his exercise in its most compressed and least distant form. They knew each other very well—so well that they could sit now in that soothing silence which is the very highest development of companionship.

"Have some whisky," said Abercrombie Smith at last between two cloudbursts. "Scotch in the jug and Irish in the bottle."

"No, thanks. I'm in for the sculls. I don't liquor when I'm training. How about you?"

"I'm reading hard. I think it best to leave it alone."

Hastie nodded, and they relapsed into a contented silence.

"By-the-way, Smith," asked Hastie, presently, "have you made the acquaintance of either of the fellows on your stair yet?"

"Just a nod when we pass. Nothing more."

"Hum! I should be inclined to let it stand at that. I know something of them both. Not much, but as much as I want. I don't think I should take them to my bosom if I were you. Not that there's much amiss with Monkhouse Lee."

"Meaning the thin one?"

"Precisely. He is a gentlemanly little fellow. I don't think there is any vice in him. But then you can't know him without knowing Bellingham."

"Meaning the fat one?"

"Yes, the fat one. And he's a man whom I, for one, would rather not know."

Abercrombie Smith raised his eyebrows and glanced across at his companion.

"What's up, then?" he asked. "Drink? Cards? Cad? You used not to be censorious."

"Ah! you evidently don't know the man, or you wouldn't ask. There's something damnable about him—something reptilian. My gorge always rises at him. I should put him down as a man with secret vices—an evil liver. He's no fool, though. They say that he is one of the best men in his line that they have ever had in the college."

"Medicine or classics?"

"Eastern languages. He's a demon at them. Chillingworth met him somewhere above the second cataract last long, and he told me that he just prattled to the Arabs as if he had been born and nursed and weaned among them. He talked Coptic to the Copts, and Hebrew to the Jews, and Arabic to the Bedouins, and they were all ready to kiss the hem of his frock-coat. There are some old hermit Johnnies up in those parts who sit on rocks and scowl and spit at the casual stranger. Well, when they saw this chap Bellingham, before he had said five words they just lay down on their bellies and wriggled. Chillingworth said that he never saw anything like it. Bellingham seemed to take it as his right, too, and strutted about among them and talked down to them like a Dutch uncle. Pretty good for an undergrad. of Old's, wasn't it?"

"Why do you say you can't know Lee without knowing Bellingham?"

"Because Bellingham is engaged to his sister Eveline. Such a bright little girl, Smith! I know the whole family well. It's disgusting to see that brute with her. A toad and a dove, that's what they always remind me of."

Abercrombie Smith grinned and knocked his ashes out against the side of the grate.

"You show every card in your hand, old chap," said he. "What a prejudiced, green-eyed, evil-thinking old man it is! You have really nothing against the fellow except that."

"Well, I've known her ever since she was as long as that cherry-wood pipe, and I don't like to see her taking risks. And it is a risk. He looks beastly. And he has a beastly temper, a venomous temper. You remember his row with Long Norton?"

"No; you always forget that I am a freshman."

"Ah, it was last winter. Of course. Well, you know the towpath along by the river. There were several fellows going along it, Bellingham in front, when they came on an old market-woman coming the other way. It had been raining—you know what those fields are like when it has rained—and the path ran between the river and a great puddle that was nearly as broad. Well, what does this swine do but keep the path, and push the old girl into the mud, where she and her marketings came to terrible grief. It was a blackguard thing to do, and Long Norton, who is as gentle a fellow as ever stepped, told him what he thought of it. One word led to another, and it ended in Norton laying his stick across the fellow's shoulders. There was the deuce of a fuss about it, and it's a treat to see the way in which Bellingham looks at Norton when they meet now. By Jove, Smith, it's nearly eleven o'clock!"

"No hurry. Light your pipe again."

"Not I. I'm supposed to be in training. Here I've been sitting gossiping when I ought to have been safely tucked up. I'll borrow your skull, if you can share it. Williams has had mine for a month. I'll take the little bones of your ear, too, if you are sure you won't need them. Thanks very much. Never mind a bag, I can carry them very well under my arm. Good-night, my son, and take my tip as to your neighbour."

When Hastie, bearing his anatomical plunder, had clattered off down the winding stair, Abercrombie Smith hurled his pipe into the wastepaper basket, and drawing his chair nearer to the lamp, plunged into a formidable green-covered volume, adorned with great colored maps of that strange internal kingdom of which we are the hapless and helpless monarchs. Though a freshman at Oxford, the student was not so in medicine, for he had worked for four years at Glasgow and at Berlin, and this coming examination would place him finally as a member of his profession. With his firm mouth, broad forehead, and clear-cut, somewhat hard-featured face, he was a man who, if he had no brilliant talent, was yet so dogged, so patient, and so strong that he might in the end overtop a more showy genius. A man who can hold his own among Scotchmen and North Germans is not a man to be easily set back. Smith had left a name at Glasgow and at Berlin, and he was bent now upon doing as much at Oxford, if hard work and devotion could accomplish it.

He had sat reading for about an hour, and the hands of the noisy carriage clock upon the side table were rapidly closing together upon the twelve, when a sudden sound fell upon the student's ear—a sharp, rather shrill sound, like the hissing intake of a man's breath who gasps under some strong emotion. Smith laid down his book and slanted his ear to listen. There was no one on either side or above him, so that the interruption came certainly from the neighbour beneath—the same neighbour of whom Hastie had given so unsavoury an account. Smith knew him only as a flabby, pale-faced man of silent and studious habits, a man, whose lamp threw a golden bar from the old turret even after he had extinguished his own. This community in lateness had formed a certain silent bond between them. It was soothing to Smith when the hours stole on towards dawning to feel that there was another so close who set as small a value upon his sleep as he did. Even now, as his thoughts turned towards him, Smith's feelings were kindly. Hastie was a good fellow, but he was rough, strong-fibred, with no imagination or sympathy. He could not tolerate departures from what he looked upon as the model type of manliness. If a man could not be measured by a public-school standard, then he was beyond the pale with Hastie. Like so many who are themselves robust, he was apt to confuse the constitution with the character, to ascribe to want of principle what was really a want of circulation. Smith, with his stronger mind, knew his friend's habit, and made allowance for it now as his thoughts turned towards the man beneath him.

There was no return of the singular sound, and Smith was about to turn to his work once more, when suddenly there broke out in the silence of the night a hoarse cry, a positive scream—the call of a man who is moved and shaken beyond all control. Smith sprang out of his chair and dropped his book. He was a man of fairly firm fibre, but there was something in this sudden, uncontrollable shriek of horror which chilled his blood and pringled in his skin. Coming in such a place and at such an hour, it brought a thousand fantastic possibilities into his head. Should he rush down, or was it better to wait? He had all the national hatred of making a scene, and he knew so little of his neighbour that he would not lightly intrude upon his affairs. For a moment he stood in doubt and even as he balanced the matter there was a quick rattle of footsteps upon the stairs, and young Monkhouse Lee, half dressed and as white as ashes, burst into his room.

"Come down!" he gasped. "Bellingham's ill."

Abercrombie Smith followed him closely down stairs into the sitting-room which was beneath his own, and intent as he was upon the matter in hand, he could not but take an amazed glance around him as he crossed the threshold. It was such a chamber as he had never seen before—a museum rather than a study. Walls and ceiling were thickly covered with a thousand strange relics from Egypt and the East. Tall, angular figures bearing burdens or weapons stalked in an uncouth frieze round the apartments. Above were bull-headed, stork-headed, cat-headed, owl-headed statues, with viper-crowned, almond-eyed monarchs, and strange, beetle-like deities cut out of the blue Egyptian lapis lazuli. Horus and Isis and Osiris peeped down from every niche and shelf, while across the ceiling a true son of Old Nile, a great, hanging-jawed crocodile, was slung in a double noose.

In the centre of this singular chamber was a large, square table, littered with papers, bottles, and the dried leaves of some graceful, palm-like plant. These varied objects had all been heaped together in order to make room for a mummy case, which had been conveyed from the wall, as was evident from the gap there, and laid across the front of the table. The mummy itself, a horrid, black, withered thing, like a charred head on a gnarled bush, was lying half out of the case, with its clawlike hand and bony forearm resting upon the table. Propped up against the sarcophagus was an old yellow scroll of papyrus, and in front of it, in a wooden armchair, sat the owner of the room, his head thrown back, his widely-opened eyes directed in a horrified stare to the crocodile above him, and his blue, thick lips puffing loudly with every expiration.

"My God! he's dying!" cried Monkhouse Lee distractedly.

He was a slim, handsome young fellow, olive-skinned and dark-eyed, of a Spanish rather than of an English type, with a Celtic intensity of manner which contrasted with the Saxon phlegm of Abercombie Smith.

"Only a faint, I think," said the medical student. "Just give me a hand with him. You take his feet. Now on to the sofa. Can you kick all those little wooden devils off? What a litter it is! Now he will be all right if we undo his collar and give him some water. What has he been up to at all?"

"I don't know. I heard him cry out. I ran up. I know him pretty well, you know. It is very good of you to come down."

"His heart is going like a pair of castanets," said Smith, laying his hand on the breast of the unconscious man. "He seems to me to be frightened all to pieces. Chuck the water over him! What a face he has got on him!"

It was indeed a strange and most repellent face, for colour and outline were equally unnatural. It was white, not with the ordinary pallor of fear but with an absolutely bloodless white, like the under side of a sole. He was very fat, but gave the impression of having at some time been considerably fatter, for his skin hung loosely in creases and folds, and was shot with a meshwork of wrinkles. Short, stubbly brown hair bristled up from his scalp, with a pair of thick, wrinkled ears protruding on either side. His light grey eyes were still open, the pupils dilated and the balls projecting in a fixed and horrid stare. It seemed to Smith as he looked down upon him that he had never seen nature's danger signals flying so plainly upon a man's countenance, and his thoughts turned more seriously to the warning which Hastie had given him an hour before.

"What the deuce can have frightened him so?" he asked.

"It's the mummy."

"The mummy? How, then?"

"I don't know. It's beastly and morbid. I wish he would drop it. It's the second fright he has given me. It was the same last winter. I found him just like this, with that horrid thing in front of him."

"What does he want with the mummy, then?"

"Oh, he's a crank, you know. It's his hobby. He knows more about these things than any man in England. But I wish he wouldn't! Ah, he's beginning to come to."

A faint tinge of colour had begun to steal back into Bellingham's ghastly cheeks, and his eyelids shivered like a sail after a calm. He clasped and unclasped his hands, drew a long, thin breath between his teeth, and suddenly jerking up his head, threw a glance of recognition around him. As his eyes fell upon the mummy, he sprang off the sofa, seized the roll of papyrus, thrust it into a drawer, turned the key, and then staggered back on to the sofa.

"What's up?" he asked. "What do you chaps want?"

"You've been shrieking out and making no end of a fuss," said Monkhouse Lee. "If our neighbour here from above hadn't come down, I'm sure I don't know what I should have done with you."

"Ah, it's Abercrombie Smith," said Bellingham, glancing up at him. "How very good of you to come in! What a fool I am! Oh, my God, what a fool I am!"

He sunk his head on to his hands, and burst into peal after peal of hysterical laughter.

"Look here! Drop it!" cried Smith, shaking him roughly by the shoulder.

"Your nerves are all in a jangle. You must drop these little midnight games with mummies, or you'll be going off your chump. You're all on wires now."

"I wonder," said Bellingham, "whether you would be as cool as I am if you had seen——"

"What then?"

"Oh, nothing. I meant that I wonder if you could sit up at night with a mummy without trying your nerves. I have no doubt that you are quite right. I dare say that I have been taking it out of myself too much lately. But I am all right now. Please don't go, though. Just wait for a few minutes until I am quite myself."

"The room is very close," remarked Lee, throwing open the window and letting in the cool night air.

"It's balsamic resin," said Bellingham. He lifted up one of the dried palmate leaves from the table and frizzled it over the chimney of the lamp. It broke away into heavy smoke wreaths, and a pungent, biting odour filled the chamber. "It's the sacred plant—the plant of the priests," he remarked. "Do you know anything of Eastern languages, Smith?"

"Nothing at all. Not a word."

The answer seemed to lift a weight from the Egyptologist's mind.

"By-the-way," he continued, "how long was it from the time that you ran down, until I came to my senses?"

"Not long. Some four or five minutes."

"I thought it could not be very long," said he, drawing a long breath. "But what a strange thing unconsciousness is! There is no measurement to it. I could not tell from my own sensations if it were seconds or weeks. Now that gentleman on the table was packed up in the days of the eleventh dynasty, some forty centuries ago, and yet if he could find his tongue he would tell us that this lapse of time has been but a closing of the eyes and a reopening of them. He is a singularly fine mummy, Smith."

Smith stepped over to the table and looked down with a professional eye at the black and twisted form in front of him. The features, though horribly discoloured, were perfect, and two little nut-like eyes still lurked in the depths of the black, hollow sockets. The blotched skin was drawn tightly from bone to bone, and a tangled wrap of black coarse hair fell over the ears. Two thin teeth, like those of a rat, overlay the shrivelled lower lip. In its crouching position, with bent joints and craned head, there was a suggestion of energy about the horrid thing which made Smith's gorge rise. The gaunt ribs, with their parchment-like covering, were exposed, and the sunken, leaden-hued abdomen, with the long slit where the embalmer had left his mark; but the lower limbs were wrapt round with coarse yellow bandages. A number of little clove-like pieces of myrrh and of cassia were sprinkled over the body, and lay scattered on the inside of the case.

"I don't know his name," said Bellingham, passing his hand over the shrivelled head. "You see the outer sarcophagus with the inscriptions is missing. Lot 249 is all the title he has now. You see it printed on his case. That was his number in the auction at which I picked him up."

"He has been a very pretty sort of fellow in his day," remarked Abercrombie Smith.

"He has been a giant. His mummy is six feet seven in length, and that would be a giant over there, for they were never a very robust race. Feel these great knotted bones, too. He would be a nasty fellow to tackle."

"Perhaps these very hands helped to build the stones into the pyramids," suggested Monkhouse Lee, looking down with disgust in his eyes at the crooked, unclean talons.

"No fear. This fellow has been pickled in natron, and looked after in the most approved style. They did not serve hodsmen in that fashion. Salt or bitumen was enough for them. It has been calculated that this sort of thing cost about seven hundred and thirty pounds in our money. Our friend was a noble at the least. What do you make of that small inscription near his feet, Smith?"

"I told you that I know no Eastern tongue."

"Ah, so you did. It is the name of the embalmer, I take it. A very conscientious worker he must have been. I wonder how many modern works will survive four thousand years?"

He kept on speaking lightly and rapidly, but it was evident to Abercrombie Smith that he was still palpitating with fear. His hands shook, his lower lip trembled, and look where he would, his eye always came sliding round to his gruesome companion. Through all his fear, however, there was a suspicion of triumph in his tone and manner. His eye shone, and his footstep, as he paced the room, was brisk and jaunty. He gave the impression of a man who has gone through an ordeal, the marks of which he still bears upon him, but which has helped him to his end.

"You're not going yet?" he cried, as Smith rose from the sofa.

At the prospect of solitude, his fears seemed to crowd back upon him, and he stretched out a hand to detain him.

"Yes, I must go. I have my work to do. You are all right now. I think that with your nervous system you should take up some less morbid study."

"Oh, I am not nervous as a rule; and I have unwrapped mummies before."

"You fainted last time," observed Monkhouse Lee.

"Ah, yes, so I did. Well, I must have a nerve tonic or a course of electricity. You are not going, Lee?"

"I'll do whatever you wish, Ned."

"Then I'll come down with you and have a shake-down on your sofa. Good-night, Smith. I am so sorry to have disturbed you with my foolishness."

They shook hands, and as the medical student stumbled up the spiral and irregular stair he heard a key turn in a door, and the steps of his two new acquaintances as they descended to the lower floor.

In this strange way began the acquaintance between Edward Bellingham and Abercrombie Smith, an acquaintance which the latter, at least, had no desire to push further. Bellingham, however, appeared to have taken a fancy to his rough-spoken neighbour, and made his advances in such a way that he could hardly be repulsed without absolute brutality. Twice he called to thank Smith for his assistance, and many times afterwards he looked in with books, papers, and such other civilities as two bachelor neighbours can offer each other. He was, as Smith soon found, a man of wide reading, with catholic tastes and an extraordinary memory. His manner, too, was so pleasing and suave that one came, after a time, to overlook his repellent appearance. For a jaded and wearied man he was no unpleasant companion, and Smith found himself, after a time, looking forward to his visits, and even returning them.

Clever as he undoubtedly was, however, the medical student seemed to detect a dash of insanity in the man. He broke out at times into a high, inflated style of talk which was in contrast with the simplicity of his life.

"It is a wonderful thing," he cried, "to feel that one can command powers of good and of evil—a ministering angel or a demon of vengeance." And again, of Monkhouse Lee, he said,—"Lee is a good fellow, an honest fellow, but he is without strength or ambition. He would not make a fit partner for a man with a great enterprise. He would not make a fit partner for me."

At such hints and innuendoes stolid Smith, puffing solemnly at his pipe, would simply raise his eyebrows and shake his head, with little interjections of medical wisdom as to earlier hours and fresher air.

One habit Bellingham had developed of late which Smith knew to be a frequent herald of a weakening mind. He appeared to be forever talking to himself. At late hours of the night, when there could be no visitor with him, Smith could still hear his voice beneath him in a low, muffled monologue, sunk almost to a whisper, and yet very audible in the silence. This solitary babbling annoyed and distracted the student, so that he spoke more than once to his neighbour about it. Bellingham, however, flushed up at the charge, and denied curtly that he had uttered a sound; indeed, he showed more annoyance over the matter than the occasion seemed to demand.

Had Abercrombie Smith had any doubt as to his own ears he had not to go far to find corroboration. Tom Styles, the little wrinkled man-servant who had attended to the wants of the lodgers in the turret for a longer time than any man's memory could carry him, was sorely put to it over the same matter.

"If you please, sir," said he, as he tidied down the top chamber one morning, "do you think Mr. Bellingham is all right, sir?"

"All right, Styles?"

"Yes sir. Right in his head, sir."

"Why should he not be, then?"

"Well, I don't know, sir. His habits has changed of late. He's not the same man he used to be, though I make free to say that he was never quite one of my gentlemen, like Mr. Hastie or yourself, sir. He's took to talkin' to himself something awful. I wonder it don't disturb you. I don't know what to make of him, sir."

"I don't know what business it is of yours, Styles."

"Well, I takes an interest, Mr. Smith. It may be forward of me, but I can't help it. I feel sometimes as if I was mother and father to my young gentlemen. It all falls on me when things go wrong and the relations come. But Mr. Bellingham, sir. I want to know what it is that walks about his room sometimes when he's out and when the door's locked on the outside."

"Eh! you're talking nonsense, Styles."

"Maybe so, sir; but I heard it more'n once with my own ears."

"Rubbish, Styles."

"Very good, sir. You'll ring the bell if you want me."

Abercrombie Smith gave little heed to the gossip of the old man-servant, but a small incident occurred a few days later which left an unpleasant effect upon his mind, and brought the words of Styles forcibly to his memory.

Bellingham had come up to see him late one night, and was entertaining him with an interesting account of the rock tombs of Beni Hassan in Upper Egypt, when Smith, whose hearing was remarkably acute, distinctly heard the sound of a door opening on the landing below.

"There's some fellow gone in or out of your room," he remarked.

Bellingham sprang up and stood helpless for a moment, with the expression of a man who is half incredulous and half afraid.

"I surely locked it. I am almost positive that I locked it," he stammered. "No one could have opened it."

"Why, I hear someone coming up the steps now," said Smith.

Bellingham rushed out through the door, slammed it loudly behind him, and hurried down the stairs. About half-way down Smith heard him stop, and thought he caught the sound of whispering. A moment later the door beneath him shut, a key creaked in a lock, and Bellingham, with beads of moisture upon his pale face, ascended the stairs once more, and re-entered the room.

"It's all right," he said, throwing himself down in a chair. "It was that fool of a dog. He had pushed the door open. I don't know how I came to forget to lock it."

"I didn't know you kept a dog," said Smith, looking very thoughtfully at the disturbed face of his companion.

"Yes, I haven't had him long. I must get rid of him. He's a great nuisance."

"He must be, if you find it so hard to shut him up. I should have thought that shutting the door would have been enough, without locking it."

"I want to prevent old Styles from letting him out. He's of some value, you know, and it would be awkward to lose him."

"I am a bit of a dog-fancier myself," said Smith, still gazing hard at his companion from the corner of his eyes. "Perhaps you'll let me have a look at it."

"Certainly. But I am afraid it cannot be to-night; I have an appointment. Is that clock right? Then I am a quarter of an hour late already. You'll excuse me, I am sure."

He picked up his cap and hurried from the room. In spite of his appointment, Smith heard him re-enter his own chamber and lock his door upon the inside.

This interview left a disagreeable impression upon the medical student's mind. Bellingham had lied to him, and lied so clumsily that it looked as if he had desperate reasons for concealing the truth. Smith knew that his neighbour had no dog. He knew, also, that the step which he had heard upon the stairs was not the step of an animal. But if it were not, then what could it be? There was old Styles's statement about the something which used to pace the room at times when the owner was absent. Could it be a woman? Smith rather inclined to the view. If so, it would mean disgrace and expulsion to Bellingham if it were discovered by the authorities, so that his anxiety and falsehoods might be accounted for. And yet it was inconceivable that an undergraduate could keep a woman in his rooms without being instantly detected. Be the explanation what it might, there was something ugly about it, and Smith determined, as he turned to his books, to discourage all further attempts at intimacy on the part of his soft-spoken and ill-favoured neighbour.

But his work was destined to interruption that night. He had hardly caught tip the broken threads when a firm, heavy footfall came three steps at a time from below, and Hastie, in blazer and flannels, burst into the room.

"Still at it!" said he, plumping down into his wonted arm-chair. "What a chap you are to stew! I believe an earthquake might come and knock Oxford into a cocked hat, and you would sit perfectly placid with your books among the rains. However, I won't bore you long. Three whiffs of baccy, and I am off."

"What's the news, then?" asked Smith, cramming a plug of bird's-eye into his briar with his forefinger.

"Nothing very much. Wilson made 70 for the freshmen against the eleven. They say that they will play him instead of Buddicomb, for Buddicomb is clean off colour. He used to be able to bowl a little, but it's nothing but half-vollies and long hops now."

"Medium right," suggested Smith, with the intense gravity which comes upon a 'varsity man when he speaks of athletics.

"Inclining to fast, with a work from leg. Comes with the arm about three inches or so. He used to be nasty on a wet wicket. Oh, by-the-way, have you heard about Long Norton?"

"What's that?"

"He's been attacked."

"Attacked?"

"Yes, just as he was turning out of the High Street, and within a hundred yards of the gate of Old's."

"But who——"

"Ah, that's the rub! If you said 'what,' you would be more grammatical. Norton swears that it was not human, and, indeed, from the scratches on his throat, I should be inclined to agree with him."

"What, then? Have we come down to spooks?"

Abercrombie Smith puffed his scientific contempt.

"Well, no; I don't think that is quite the idea, either. I am inclined to think that if any showman has lost a great ape lately, and the brute is in these parts, a jury would find a true bill against it. Norton passes that way every night, you know, about the same hour. There's a tree that hangs low over the path—the big elm from Rainy's garden. Norton thinks the thing dropped on him out of the tree. Anyhow, he was nearly strangled by two arms, which, he says, were as strong and as thin as steel bands. He saw nothing; only those beastly arms that tightened and tightened on him. He yelled his head nearly off, and a couple of chaps came running, and the thing went over the wall like a cat. He never got a fair sight of it the whole time. It gave Norton a shake up, I can tell you. I tell him it has been as good as a change at the sea-side for him."

"A garrotter, most likely," said Smith.

"Very possibly. Norton says not; but we don't mind what he says. The garrotter had long nails, and was pretty smart at swinging himself over walls. By-the-way, your beautiful neighbour would be pleased if he heard about it. He had a grudge against Norton, and he's not a man, from what I know of him, to forget his little debts. But hallo, old chap, what have you got in your noddle?"

"Nothing," Smith answered curtly.

He had started in his chair, and the look had flashed over his face which comes upon a man who is struck suddenly by some unpleasant idea.

"You looked as if something I had said had taken you on the raw. By-the-way, you have made the acquaintance of Master B. since I looked in last, have you not? Young Monkhouse Lee told me something to that effect."

"Yes; I know him slightly. He has been up here once or twice."

"Well, you're big enough and ugly enough to take care of yourself. He's not what I should call exactly a healthy sort of Johnny, though, no doubt, he's very clever, and all that. But you'll soon find out for yourself. Lee is all right; he's a very decent little fellow. Well, so long, old chap! I row Mullins for the Vice-Chancellor's pot on Wednesday week, so mind you come down, in case I don't see you before."

Bovine Smith laid down his pipe and turned stolidly to his books once more. But with all the will in the world, he found it very hard to keep his mind upon his work. It would slip away to brood upon the man beneath him, and upon the little mystery which hung round his chambers. Then his thoughts turned to this singular attack of which Hastie had spoken, and to the grudge which Bellingham was said to owe the object of it. The two ideas would persist in rising together in his mind, as though there were some close and intimate connection between them. And yet the suspicion was so dim and vague that it could not be put down in words.

"Confound the chap!" cried Smith, as he shied his book on pathology across the room. "He has spoiled my night's reading, and that's reason enough, if there were no other, why I should steer clear of him in the future."

For ten days the medical student confined himself so closely to his studies that he neither saw nor heard anything of either of the men beneath him. At the hours when Bellingham had been accustomed to visit him, he took care to sport his oak, and though he more than once heard a knocking at his outer door, he resolutely refused to answer it. One afternoon, however, he was descending the stairs when, just as he was passing it, Bellingham's door flew open, and young Monkhouse Lee came out with his eyes sparkling and a dark flush of anger upon his olive cheeks. Close at his heels followed Bellingham, his fat, unhealthy face all quivering with malignant passion.

"You fool!" he hissed. "You'll be sorry."

"Very likely," cried the other. "Mind what I say. It's off! I won't hear of it!"

"You've promised, anyhow."

"Oh, I'll keep that! I won't speak. But I'd rather little Eva was in her grave. Once for all, it's off. She'll do what I say. We don't want to see you again."

So much Smith could not avoid hearing, but he hurried on, for he had no wish to be involved in their dispute. There had been a serious breach between them, that was clear enough, and Lee was going to cause the engagement with his sister to be broken off. Smith thought of Hastie's comparison of the toad and the dove, and was glad to think that the matter was at an end. Bellingham's face when he was in a passion was not pleasant to look upon. He was not a man to whom an innocent girl could be trusted for life. As he walked, Smith wondered languidly what could have caused the quarrel, and what the promise might be which Bellingham had been so anxious that Monkhouse Lee should keep.

It was the day of the sculling match between Hastie and Mullins, and a stream of men were making their way down to the banks of the Isis. A May sun was shining brightly, and the yellow path was barred with the black shadows of the tall elm-trees. On either side the grey colleges lay back from the road, the hoary old mothers of minds looking out from their high, mullioned windows at the tide of young life which swept so merrily past them. Black-clad tutors, prim officials, pale reading men, brown-faced, straw-hatted young athletes in white sweaters or many-coloured blazers, all were hurrying towards the blue winding river which curves through the Oxford meadows.

Abercrombie Smith, with the intuition of an old oarsman, chose his position at the point where he knew that the struggle, if there were a struggle, would come. Far off he heard the hum which announced the start, the gathering roar of the approach, the thunder of running feet, and the shouts of the men in the boats beneath him. A spray of half-clad, deep-breathing runners shot past him, and craning over their shoulders, he saw Hastie pulling a steady thirty-six, while his opponent, with a jerky forty, was a good boat's length behind him. Smith gave a cheer for his friend, and pulling out his watch, was starting off again for his chambers, when he felt a touch upon his shoulder, and found that young Monkhouse Lee was beside him.

"I saw you there," he said, in a timid, deprecating way. "I wanted to speak to you, if you could spare me a half-hour. This cottage is mine. I share it with Harrington of King's. Come in and have a cup of tea."

"I must be back presently," said Smith. "I am hard on the grind at present. But I'll come in for a few minutes with pleasure. I wouldn't have come out only Hastie is a friend of mine."

"So he is of mine. Hasn't he a beautiful style? Mullins wasn't in it. But come into the cottage. It's a little den of a place, but it is pleasant to work in during the summer months."

It was a small, square, white building, with green doors and shutters, and a rustic trellis-work porch, standing back some fifty yards from the river's bank. Inside, the main room was roughly fitted up as a study—deal table, unpainted shelves with books, and a few cheap oleographs upon the wall. A kettle sang upon a spirit-stove, and there were tea things upon a tray on the table.

"Try that chair and have a cigarette," said Lee. "Let me pour you out a cup of tea. It's so good of you to come in, for I know that your time is a good deal taken up. I wanted to say to you that, if I were you, I should change my rooms at once."

"Eh?"

Smith sat staring with a lighted match in one hand and his unlit cigarette in the other.

"Yes; it must seem very extraordinary, and the worst of it is that I cannot give my reasons, for I am under a solemn promise—a very solemn promise. But I may go so far as to say that I don't think Bellingham is a very safe man to live near. I intend to camp out here as much as I can for a time."

"Not safe! What do you mean?"

"Ah, that's what I mustn't say. But do take my advice, and move your rooms. We had a grand row to-day. You must have heard us, for you came down the stairs."

"I saw that you had fallen out."

"He's a horrible chap, Smith. That is the only word for him. I have had doubts about him ever since that night when he fainted—you remember, when you came down. I taxed him to-day, and he told me things that made my hair rise, and wanted me to stand in with him. I'm not strait-laced, but I am a clergyman's son, you know, and I think there are some things which are quite beyond the pale. I only thank God that I found him out before it was too late, for he was to have married into my family."

"This is all very fine, Lee," said Abercrombie Smith curtly. "But either you are saying a great deal too much or a great deal too little."

"I give you a warning."

"If there is real reason for warning, no promise can bind you. If I see a rascal about to blow a place up with dynamite no pledge will stand in my way of preventing him."

"Ah, but I cannot prevent him, and I can do nothing but warn you."

"Without saying what you warn me against."

"Against Bellingham."

"But that is childish. Why should I fear him, or any man?"

"I can't tell you. I can only entreat you to change your rooms. You are in danger where you are. I don't even say that Bellingham would wish to injure you. But it might happen, for he is a dangerous neighbour just now."

"Perhaps I know more than you think," said Smith, looking keenly at the young man's boyish, earnest face. "Suppose I tell you that some one else shares Bellingham's rooms."

Monkhouse Lee sprang from his chair in uncontrollable excitement.

"You know, then?" he gasped.

"A woman."

Lee dropped back again with a groan.

"My lips are sealed," he said. "I must not speak."

"Well, anyhow," said Smith, rising, "it is not likely that I should allow myself to be frightened out of rooms which suit me very nicely. It would be a little too feeble for me to move out all my goods and chattels because you say that Bellingham might in some unexplained way do me an injury. I think that I'll just take my chance, and stay where I am, and as I see that it's nearly five o'clock, I must ask you to excuse me."

He bade the young student adieu in a few curt words, and made his way homeward through the sweet spring evening feeling half-ruffled, half-amused, as any other strong, unimaginative man might who has been menaced by a vague and shadowy danger.

There was one little indulgence which Abercrombie Smith always allowed himself, however closely his work might press upon him. Twice a week, on the Tuesday and the Friday, it was his invariable custom to walk over to Farlingford, the residence of Dr. Plumptree Peterson, situated about a mile and a half out of Oxford. Peterson had been a close friend of Smith's elder brother Francis, and as he was a bachelor, fairly well-to-do, with a good cellar and a better library, his house was a pleasant goal for a man who was in need of a brisk walk. Twice a week, then, the medical student would swing out there along the dark country roads, and spend a pleasant hour in Peterson's comfortable study, discussing, over a glass of old port, the gossip of the 'varsity or the latest developments of medicine or of surgery.

On the day which followed his interview with Monkhouse Lee, Smith shut up his books at a quarter past eight, the hour when he usually started for his friend's house. As he was leaving his room, however, his eyes chanced to fall upon one of the books which Bellingham had lent him, and his conscience pricked him for not having returned it. However repellent the man might be, he should not be treated with discourtesy. Taking the book, he walked downstairs and knocked at his neighbour's door. There was no answer; but on turning the handle he found that it was unlocked. Pleased at the thought of avoiding an interview, he stepped inside, and placed the book with his card upon the table.

The lamp was turned half down, but Smith could see the details of the room plainly enough. It was all much as he had seen it before—the frieze, the animal-headed gods, the banging crocodile, and the table littered over with papers and dried leaves. The mummy case stood upright against the wall, but the mummy itself was missing. There was no sign of any second occupant of the room, and he felt as he withdrew that he had probably done Bellingham an injustice. Had he a guilty secret to preserve, he would hardly leave his door open so that all the world might enter.

The spiral stair was as black as pitch, and Smith was slowly making his way down its irregular steps, when he was suddenly conscious that something had passed him in the darkness. There was a faint sound, a whiff of air, a light brushing past his elbow, but so slight that he could scarcely be certain of it. He stopped and listened, but the wind was rustling among the ivy outside, and he could hear nothing else.

"Is that you, Styles?" he shouted.

There was no answer, and all was still behind him. It must have been a sudden gust of air, for there were crannies and cracks in the old turret. And yet he could almost have sworn that he heard a footfall by his very side. He had emerged into the quadrangle, still turning the matter over in his head, when a man came running swiftly across the smooth-cropped lawn.

"Is that you, Smith?"

"Hullo, Hastie!"

"For God's sake come at once! Young Lee is drowned! Here's Harrington of King's with the news. The doctor is out. You'll do, but come along at once. There may be life in him."

"Have you brandy?"

"No."

"I'll bring some. There's a flask on my table."

Smith bounded up the stairs, taking three at a time, seized the flask, and was rushing down with it, when, as he passed Bellingham's room, his eyes fell upon something which left him gasping and staring upon the landing.

The door, which he had closed behind him, was now open, and right in front of him, with the lamp-light shining upon it, was the mummy case. Three minutes ago it had been empty. He could swear to that. Now it framed the lank body of its horrible occupant, who stood, grim and stark, with his black shrivelled face towards the door. The form was lifeless and inert, but it seemed to Smith as he gazed that there still lingered a lurid spark of vitality, some faint sign of consciousness in the little eyes which lurked in the depths of the hollow sockets. So astounded and shaken was he that he had forgotten his errand, and was still staring at the lean, sunken figure when the voice of his friend below recalled him to himself.

"Come on, Smith!" he shouted. "It's life and death, you know. Hurry up! Now, then," he added, as the medical student reappeared, "let us do a sprint. It is well under a mile, and we should do it in five minutes. A human life is better worth running for than a pot."

Neck and neck they dashed through the darkness, and did not pull up until, panting and spent, they had reached the little cottage by the river. Young Lee, limp and dripping like a broken water-plant, was stretched upon the sofa, the green scum of the river upon his black hair, and a fringe of white foam upon his leaden-hued lips. Beside him knelt his fellow-student Harrington, endeavouring to chafe some warmth back into his rigid limbs.

"I think there's life in him," said Smith, with his hand to the lad's side. "Put your watch glass to his lips. Yes, there's dimming on it. You take one arm, Hastie. Now work it as I do, and we'll soon pull him round."

For ten minutes they worked in silence, inflating and depressing the chest of the unconscious man. At the end of that time a shiver ran through his body, his lips trembled, and he opened his eyes. The three students burst out into an irrepressible cheer.

"Wake up, old chap. You've frightened us quite enough."

"Have some brandy. Take a sip from the flask."

"He's all right now," said his companion Harrington. "Heavens, what a fright I got! I was reading here, and he had gone for a stroll as far as the river, when I heard a scream and a splash. Out I ran, and by the time that I could find him and fish him out, all life seemed to have gone. Then Simpson couldn't get a doctor, for he has a game-leg, and I had to run, and I don't know what I'd have done without you fellows. That's right, old chap. Sit up."

Monkhouse Lee had raised himself on his hands, and looked wildly about him.

"What's up?" he asked. "I've been in the water. Ah, yes; I remember."

A look of fear came into his eyes, and he sank his face into his hands.

"How did you fall in?"

"I didn't fall in."

"How, then?"

"I was thrown in. I was standing by the bank, and something from behind picked me up like a feather and hurled me in. I heard nothing, and I saw nothing. But I know what it was, for all that."

"And so do I," whispered Smith.

Lee looked up with a quick glance of surprise. "You've learned, then!" he said. "You remember the advice I gave you?"

"Yes, and I begin to think that I shall take it."

"I don't know what the deuce you fellows are talking about," said Hastie, "but I think, if I were you, Harrington, I should get Lee to bed at once. It will be time enough to discuss the why and the wherefore when he is a little stronger. I think, Smith, you and I can leave him alone now. I am walking back to college; if you are coming in that direction, we can have a chat."

But it was little chat that they had upon their homeward path. Smith's mind was too full of the incidents of the evening, the absence of the mummy from his neighbour's rooms, the step that passed him on the stair, the reappearance —the extraordinary, inexplicable reappearance of the grisly thing—and then this attack upon Lee, corresponding so closely to the previous outrage upon another man against whom Bellingham bore a grudge. All this settled in his thoughts, together with the many little incidents which had previously turned him against his neighbour, and the singular circumstances under which he was first called in to him. What had been a dim suspicion, a vague, fantastic conjecture, had suddenly taken form, and stood out in his mind as a grim fact, a thing not to be denied. And yet, how monstrous it was! how unheard of! how entirely beyond all bounds of human experience. An impartial judge, or even the friend who walked by his side, would simply tell him that his eyes had deceived him, that the mummy had been there all the time, that young Lee had tumbled into the river as any other man tumbles into a river, and that a blue pill was the best thing for a disordered liver. He felt that he would have said as much if the positions had been reversed. And yet he could swear that Bellingham was a murderer at heart, and that he wielded a weapon such as no man had ever used in all the grim history of crime.

Hastie had branched off to his rooms with a few crisp and emphatic comments upon his friend's unsociability, and Abercrombie Smith crossed the quadrangle to his corner turret with a strong feeling of repulsion for his chambers and their associations. He would take Lee's advice, and move his quarters as soon as possible, for how could a man study when his ear was ever straining for every murmur or footstep in the room below? He observed, as he crossed over the lawn, that the light was still shining in Bellingham's window, and as he passed up the staircase the door opened, and the man himself looked out at him. With his fat, evil face he was like some bloated spider fresh from the weaving of his poisonous web.

"Good-evening," said he. "Won't you come in?"

"No," cried Smith, fiercely.

"No? You are busy as ever? I wanted to ask you about Lee. I was sorry to hear that there was a rumour that something was amiss with him."

His features were grave, but there was the gleam of a hidden laugh in his eyes as he spoke. Smith saw it, and he could have knocked him down for it.

"You'll be sorrier still to hear that Monkhouse Lee is doing very well, and is out of all danger," he answered. "Your hellish tricks have not come off this time. Oh, you needn't try to brazen it out. I know all about it."

Bellingham took a step back from the angry student, and half-closed the door as if to protect himself.

"You are mad," he said. "What do you mean? Do you assert that I had anything to do with Lee's accident?"

"Yes," thundered Smith. "You and that bag of bones behind you; you worked it between you. I tell you what it is, Master B., they have given up burning folk like you, but we still keep a hangman, and, by George! if any man in this college meets his death while you are here, I'll have you up, and if you don't swing for it, it won't be my fault. You'll find that your filthy Egyptian tricks won't answer in England."

"You're a raving lunatic," said Bellingham.

"All right. You just remember what I say, for you'll find that I'll be better than my word."

The door slammed, and Smith went fuming up to his chamber, where he locked the door upon the inside, and spent half the night in smoking his old briar and brooding over the strange events of the evening.

Next morning Abercrombie Smith heard nothing of his neighbour, but Harrington called upon him in the afternoon to say that Lee was almost himself again. All day Smith stuck fast to his work, but in the evening he determined to pay the visit to his friend Dr. Peterson upon which he had started upon the night before. A good walk and a friendly chat would be welcome to his jangled nerves.

Bellingham's door was shut as he passed, but glancing back when he was some distance from the turret, he saw his neighbour's head at the window outlined against the lamp-light, his face pressed apparently against the glass as he gazed out into the darkness. It was a blessing to be away from all contact with him, but if for a few hours, and Smith stepped out briskly, and breathed the soft spring air into his lungs. The half-moon lay in the west between two Gothic pinnacles, and threw upon the silvered street a dark tracery from the stone-work above. There was a brisk breeze, and light, fleecy clouds drifted swiftly across the sky. Old's was on the very border of the town, and in five minutes Smith found himself beyond the houses and between the hedges of a May-scented Oxfordshire lane.

It was a lonely and little frequented road which led to his friend's house. Early as it was, Smith did not meet a single soul upon his way. He walked briskly along until he came to the avenue gate, which opened into the long gravel drive leading up to Farlingford. In front of him he could see the cosy red light of the windows glimmering through the foliage. He stood with his hand upon the iron latch of the swinging gate, and he glanced back at the road along which he had come. Something was coming swiftly down it.

It moved in the shadow of the hedge, silently and furtively, a dark, crouching figure, dimly visible against the black background. Even as he gazed back at it, it had lessened its distance by twenty paces, and was fast closing upon him. Out of the darkness he had a glimpse of a scraggy neck, and of two eyes that will ever haunt him in his dreams. He turned, and with a cry of terror he ran for his life up the avenue. There were the red lights, the signals of safety, almost within a stone's throw of him. He was a famous runner, but never had he run as he ran that night.

The heavy gate had swung into place behind him, but he heard it dash open again before his pursuer. As he rushed madly and wildly through the night, he could hear a swift, dry patter behind him, and could see, as he threw back a glance, that this horror was bounding like a tiger at his heels, with blazing eyes and one stringy arm outthrown. Thank God, the door was ajar. He could see the thin bar of light which shot from the lamp in the hall. Nearer yet sounded the clatter from behind. He heard a hoarse gurgling at his very shoulder. With a shriek he flung himself against the door, slammed and bolted it behind him, and sank half-fainting on to the hall chair.

"My goodness, Smith, what's the matter?" asked Peterson, appearing at the door of his study.

"Give me some brandy!"

Peterson disappeared, and came rushing out again with a glass and a decanter.

"You need it," he said, as his visitor drank off what he poured out for him. "Why, man, you are as white as a cheese."

Smith laid down his glass, rose up, and took a deep breath.

"I am my own man again now," said he. "I was never so unmanned before. But, with your leave, Peterson, I will sleep here to-night, for I don't think I could face that road again except by daylight. It's weak, I know, but I can't help it."

Peterson looked at his visitor with a very questioning eye.

"Of course you shall sleep here if you wish. I'll tell Mrs. Burney to make up the spare bed. Where are you off to now?"

"Come up with me to the window that overlooks the door. I want you to see what I have seen."

They went up to the window of the upper hall whence they could look down upon the approach to the house. The drive and the fields on either side lay quiet and still, bathed in the peaceful moonlight.

"Well, really, Smith," remarked Peterson, "it is well that I know you to be an abstemious man. What in the world can have frightened you?"

"I'll tell you presently. But where can it have gone? Ah, now look, look! See the curve of the road just beyond your gate."

"Yes, I see; you needn't pinch my arm off. I saw someone pass. I should say a man, rather thin, apparently, and tall, very tall. But what of him? And what of yourself? You are still shaking like an aspen leaf."

"I have been within hand-grip of the devil, that's all. But come down to your study, and I shall tell you the whole story."

He did so. Under the cheery lamplight, with a glass of wine on the table beside him, and the portly form and florid face of his friend in front, he narrated, in their order, all the events, great and small, which had formed so singular a chain, from the night on which he had found Bellingham fainting in front of the mummy case until his horrid experience of an hour ago.

"There now," he said as he concluded, "that's the whole black business. It is monstrous and incredible, but it is true."

Dr. Plumptree Peterson sat for some time in silence with a very puzzled expression upon his face.

"I never heard of such a thing in my life, never!" he said at last. "You have told me the facts. Now tell me your inferences."

"You can draw your own."

"But I should like to hear yours. You have thought over the matter, and I have not."

"Well, it must be a little vague in detail, but the main points seem to me to be clear enough. This fellow Bellingham, in his Eastern studies, has got hold of some infernal secret by which a mummy—or possibly only this particular mummy—can be temporarily brought to life. He was trying this disgusting business on the night when he fainted. No doubt the sight of the creature moving had shaken his nerve, even though he had expected it. You remember that almost the first words he said were to call out upon himself as a fool. Well, he got more hardened afterwards, and carried the matter through without fainting. The vitality which he could put into it was evidently only a passing thing, for I have seen it continually in its case as dead as this table. He has some elaborate process, I fancy, by which he brings the thing to pass. Having done it, he naturally bethought him that he might use the creature as an agent. It has intelligence and it has strength. For some purpose he took Lee into his confidence; but Lee, like a decent Christian, would have nothing to do with such a business. Then they had a row, and Lee vowed that he would tell his sister of Bellingham's true character. Bellingham's game was to prevent him, and he nearly managed it, by setting this creature of his on his track. He had already tried its powers upon another man—Norton—towards whom he had a grudge. It is the merest chance that he has not two murders upon his soul. Then, when I taxed him with the matter, he had the strongest reasons for wishing to get me out of the way before I could convey my knowledge to anyone else. He got his chance when I went out, for he knew my habits, and where I was bound for. I have had a narrow shave, Peterson, and it is mere luck you didn't find me on your doorstep in the morning. I'm not a nervous man as a rule, and I never thought to have the fear of death put upon me as it was to-night."

"My dear boy, you take the matter too seriously," said his companion. "Your nerves are out of order with your work, and you make too much of it. How could such a thing as this stride about the streets of Oxford, even at night, without being seen?"

"It has been seen. There is quite a scare in the town about an escaped ape, as they imagine the creature to be. It is the talk of the place."

"Well, it's a striking chain of events. And yet, my dear fellow, you must allow that each incident in itself is capable of a more natural explanation."

"What! even my adventure of to-night?"

"Certainly. You come out with your nerves all unstrung, and your head full of this theory of yours. Some gaunt, half-famished tramp steals after you, and seeing you run, is emboldened to pursue you. Your fears and imagination do the rest."

"It won't do, Peterson; it won't do."

"And again, in the instance of your finding the mummy case empty, and then a few moments later with an occupant, you know that it was lamplight, that the lamp was half turned down, and that you had no special reason to look hard at the case. It is quite possible that you may have overlooked the creature in the first instance."

"No, no; it is out of the question."

"And then Lee may have fallen into the river, and Norton been garrotted. It is certainly a formidable indictment that you have against Bellingham; but if you were to place it before a police magistrate, he would simply laugh in your face."

"I know he would. That is why I mean to take the matter into my own hands."

"Eh?"

"Yes; I feel that a public duty rests upon me, and, besides, I must do it for my own safety, unless I choose to allow myself to be hunted by this beast out of the college, and that would be a little too feeble. I have quite made up my mind what I shall do. And first of all, may I use your paper and pens for an hour?"

"Most certainly. You will find all that you want upon that side table."

Abercrombie Smith sat down before a sheet of foolscap, and for an hour, and then for a second hour his pen travelled swiftly over it. Page after page was finished and tossed aside while his friend leaned back in his arm-chair, looking across at him with patient curiosity. At last, with an exclamation of satisfaction, Smith sprang to his feet, gathered his papers up into order, and laid the last one upon Peterson's desk.

"Kindly sign this as a witness," he said.

"A witness? Of what?"

"Of my signature, and of the date. The date is the most important. Why, Peterson, my life might hang upon it."

"My dear Smith, you are talking wildly. Let me beg you to go to bed."

"On the contrary, I never spoke so deliberately in my life. And I will promise to go to bed the moment you have signed it."

"But what is it?"

"It is a statement of all that I have been telling you to-night. I wish you to witness it."

"Certainly," said Peterson, signing his name under that of his companion. "There you are! But what is the idea?"

"You will kindly retain it, and produce it in case I am arrested."

"Arrested? For what?"

"For murder. It is quite on the cards. I wish to be ready for every event. There is only one course open to me, and I am determined to take it."

"For Heaven's sake, don't do anything rash!"

"Believe me, it would be far more rash to adopt any other course. I hope that we won't need to bother you, but it will ease my mind to know that you have this statement of my motives. And now I am ready to take your advice and to go to roost, for I want to be at my best in the morning."

Abercrombie Smith was not an entirely pleasant man to have as an enemy. Slow and easytempered, he was formidable when driven to action. He brought to every purpose in life the same deliberate resoluteness which had distinguished him as a scientific student. He had laid his studies aside for a day, but he intended that the day should not be wasted. Not a word did he say to his host as to his plans, but by nine o'clock he was well on his way to Oxford.

In the High Street he stopped at Clifford's, the gun-maker's, and bought a heavy revolver, with a box of central-fire cartridges. Six of them he slipped into the chambers, and half-cocking the weapon, placed it in the pocket of his coat. He then made his way to Hastie's rooms, where the big oarsman was lounging over his breakfast, with the Sporting Times propped up against the coffeepot.

"Hullo! What's up?" he asked. "Have some coffee?"

"No, thank you. I want you to come with me, Hastie, and do what I ask you."

"Certainly, my boy."

"And bring a heavy stick with you."

"Hullo!" Hastie stared. "Here's a hunting-crop that would fell an ox."

"One other thing. You have a box of amputating knives. Give me the longest of them."

"There you are. You seem to be fairly on the war trail. Anything else?"

"No; that will do." Smith placed the knife inside his coat, and led the way to the quadrangle. "We are neither of us chickens, Hastie," said he. "I think I can do this job alone, but I take you as a precaution. I am going to have a little talk with Bellingham. If I have only him to deal with, I won't, of course, need you. If I shout, however, up you come, and lam out with your whip as hard as you can lick. Do you understand?"

"All right. I'll come if I hear you bellow."

"Stay here, then. It may be a little time, but don't budge until I come down."

"I'm a fixture."

Smith ascended the stairs, opened Bellingham's door and stepped in. Bellingham was seated behind his table, writing. Beside him, among his litter of strange possessions, towered the mummy case, with its sale number 249 still stuck upon its front, and its hideous occupant stiff and stark within it. Smith looked very deliberately round him, closed the door, locked it, took the key from the inside, and then stepping across to the fireplace, struck a match and set the fire alight. Bellingham sat staring, with amazement and rage upon his bloated face.

"Well, really now, you make yourself at home," he gasped.

Smith sat himself deliberately down, placing his watch upon the table, drew out his pistol, cocked it, and laid it in his lap. Then he took the long amputating knife from his bosom, and threw it down in front of Bellingham.

"Now, then," said he, "just get to work and cut up that mummy."

"Oh, is that it?" said Bellingham with a sneer.

"Yes, that is it. They tell me that the law can't touch you. But I have a law that will set matters straight. If in five minutes you have not set to work, I swear by the God who made me that I will put a bullet through your brain!"

"You would murder me?"

Bellingham had half risen, and his face was the colour of putty.

"Yes."

"And for what?"

"To stop your mischief. One minute has gone."

"But what have I done?"

"I know and you know."

"This is mere bullying."

"Two minutes are gone."

"But you must give reasons. You are a madman—a dangerous madman. Why should I destroy my own property? It is a valuable mummy."

"You must cut it up, and you must burn it."

"I will do no such thing."

"Four minutes are gone."

Smith took up the pistol and he looked towards Bellingham with an inexorable face. As the second-hand stole round, he raised his hand, and the finger twitched upon the trigger.

"There! there! I'll do it!" screamed Bellingham.

In frantic haste he caught up the knife and hacked at the figure of the mummy, ever glancing round to see the eye and the weapon of his terrible visitor bent upon him. The creature crackled and snapped under every stab of the keen blade. A thick yellow dust rose up from it. Spices and dried essences rained down upon the floor. Suddenly, with a rending crack, its backbone snapped asunder, and it fell, a brown heap of sprawling limbs, upon the floor.

"Now into the fire!" said Smith.

The flames leaped and roared as the dried and tinderlike debris was piled upon it. The little room was like the stoke-hole of a steamer and the sweat ran down the faces of the two men; but still the one stooped and worked, while the other sat watching him with a set face. A thick, fat smoke oozed out from the fire, and a heavy smell of burned rosin and singed hair filled the air. In a quarter of an hour a few charred and brittle sticks were all that was left of Lot No. 249.

"Perhaps that will satisfy you," snarled Bellingham, with hate and fear in his little grey eyes as he glanced back at his tormenter.

"No; I must make a clean sweep of all your materials. We must have no more devil's tricks. In with all these leaves! They may have something to do with it."

"And what now?" asked Bellingham, when the leaves also had been added to the blaze.

"Now the roll of papyrus which you had on the table that night. It is in that drawer, I think."

"No, no," shouted Bellingham. "Don't burn that! Why, man, you don't know what you do. It is unique; it contains wisdom which is nowhere else to be found."

"Out with it!"

"But look here, Smith, you can't really mean it. I'll share the knowledge with you. I'll teach you all that is in it. Or, stay, let me only copy it before you burn it!"

Smith stepped forward and turned the key in the drawer. Taking out the yellow, curled roll of paper, he threw it into the fire, and pressed it down with his heel. Bellingham screamed, and grabbed at it; but Smith pushed him back, and stood over it until it was reduced to a formless grey ash.

"Now, Master B.," said he, "I think I have pretty well drawn your teeth. You'll hear from me again, if you return to your old tricks. And now good-morning, for I must go back to my studies."

And such is the narrative of Abercrombie Smith as to the singular events which occurred in Old College, Oxford, in the spring of '84. As Bellingham left the university immediately afterwards, and was last heard of in the

Soudan, there is no one who can contradict his statement. But the wisdom of men is small, and the ways of nature are strange, and who shall put a bound to the dark things which may be found by those who seek for them?

THE LOS AMIGOS FIASCO.

I used to be the leading practitioner of Los Amigos. Of course, everyone has heard of the great electrical generating gear there. The town is wide spread, and there are dozens of little townlets and villages all round, which receive their supply from the same centre, so that the works are on a very large scale. The Los Amigos folk say that they are the largest upon earth, but then we claim that for everything in Los Amigos except the gaol and the death-rate. Those are said to be the smallest.

Now, with so fine an electrical supply, it seemed to be a sinful waste of hemp that the Los Amigos criminals should perish in the old-fashioned manner. And then came the news of the eleotrocutions in the East, and how the results had not after all been so instantaneous as had been hoped. The Western Engineers raised their eyebrows when they read of the puny shocks by which these men had perished, and they vowed in Los Amigos that when an irreclaimable came their way he should be dealt handsomely by, and have the run of all the big dynamos. There should be no reserve, said the engineers, but he should have all that they had got. And what the result of that would be none could predict, save that it must be absolutely blasting and deadly. Never before had a man been so charged with electricity as they would charge him. He was to be smitten by the essence of ten thunderbolts. Some prophesied combustion, and some disintegration and disappearance. They were waiting eagerly to settle the question by actual demonstration, and it was just at that moment that Duncan Warner came that way.

Warner had been wanted by the law, and by nobody else, for many years. Desperado, murderer, train robber and road agent, he was a man beyond the pale of human pity. He had deserved a dozen deaths, and the Los Amigos folk grudged him so gaudy a one as that. He seemed to feel himself to be unworthy of it, for he made two frenzied attempts at escape. He was a powerful, muscular man, with a lion head, tangled black locks, and a sweeping beard which covered his broad chest. When he was tried, there was no finer head in all the crowded court. It's no new thing to find the best face looking from the dock. But his good looks could not balance his bad deeds. His advocate did all he knew, but the cards lay against him, and Duncan Warner was handed over to the mercy of the big Los Amigos dynamos.

I was there at the committee meeting when the matter was discussed. The town council had chosen four experts to look after the arrangements. Three of them were admirable. There was Joseph M'Conner, the very man who had designed the dynamos, and there was Joshua Westmacott, the chairman of the Los Amigos Electrical Supply Company, Limited. Then there was myself as the chief medical man, and lastly an old German of the name of Peter Stulpnagel. The Germans were a strong body at Los Amigos, and they all voted for their man. That was how he got on the committee. It was said that he had been a wonderful electrician at home, and he was eternally working with wires and insulators and Leyden jars; but, as he never seemed to get any further, or to have any results worth publishing he came at last to be regarded as a harmless crank, who had made science his hobby. We three practical men smiled when we heard that he had been elected as our colleague, and at the meeting we fixed it all up very nicely among ourselves without much thought of the old fellow who sat with his ears scooped forward in his hands, for he was a trifle hard of hearing, taking no more part in the proceedings than the gentlemen of the press who scribbled their notes on the back benches.

We did not take long to settle it all. In New York a strength of some two thousand volts had been used, and death had not been instantaneous. Evidently their shock had been too weak. Los Amigos should not fall into that error. The charge should be six times greater, and therefore, of course, it would be six times more effective. Nothing could possibly be more logical. The whole concentrated force of the great dynamos should be employed on Duncan Warner.

So we three settled it, and had already risen to break up the meeting, when our silent companion opened his month for the first time.

"Gentlemen," said he, "you appear to me to show an extraordinary ignorance upon the subject of electricity. You have not mastered the first principles of its actions upon a human being."

The committee was about to break into an angry reply to this brusque comment, but the chairman of the Electrical Company tapped his forehead to claim its indulgence for the crankiness of the speaker.

"Pray tell us, sir," said he, with an ironical smile, "what is there in our conclusions with which you find fault?"

"With your assumption that a large dose of electricity will merely increase the effect of a small dose. Do you not think it possible that it might have an entirely different result? Do you know anything, by actual experiment, of the effect of such powerful shocks?"

"We know it by analogy," said the chairman, pompously. "All drugs increase their effect when they increase their dose; for example—for example——"

"Whisky," said Joseph M'Connor.

"Quite so. Whisky. You see it there."

Peter Stulpnagel smiled and shook his head.

"Your argument is not very good," said he. "When I used to take whisky, I used to find that one glass would excite me, but that six would send me to sleep, which is just the opposite. Now, suppose that electricity were to act in just the opposite way also, what then?"

We three practical men burst out laughing. We had known that our colleague was queer, but we never had thought that he would be as queer as this.

"What then?" repeated Philip Stulpnagel.

"We'll take our chances," said the chairman.

"Pray consider," said Peter, "that workmen who have touched the wires, and who have received shocks of only a few hundred volts, have died instantly. The fact is well known. And yet when a much greater force was used upon a criminal at New York, the man struggled for some little time. Do you not clearly see that the smaller dose is the more deadly?"

"I think, gentlemen, that this discussion has been carried on quite long enough," said the chairman, rising again. "The point, I take it, has already been decided by the majority of the committee, and Duncan Warner shall be electrocuted on Tuesday by the full strength of the Los Amigos dynamos. Is it not so?"

"I agree," said Joseph M'Connor.

"I agree," said I.

"And I protest," said Peter Stulpnagel.

"Then the motion is carried, and your protest will be duly entered in the minutes," said the chairman, and so the sitting was dissolved.

The attendance at the electrocution was a very small one. We four members of the committee were, of course, present with the executioner, who was to act under their orders. The others were the United States Marshal, the governor of the gaol, the chaplain, and three members of the press. The room was a small brick chamber, forming an outhouse to the Central Electrical station. It had been used as a laundry, and had an oven and copper at one side, but no other furniture save a single chair for the condemned man. A metal plate for his feet was placed in front of it, to which ran a thick, insulated wire. Above, another wire depended from the ceiling, which could be connected with a small metallic rod projecting from a cap which was to be placed upon his head. When this connection was established Duncan Warner's hour was come.

There was a solemn hush as we waited for the coming of the prisoner. The practical engineers looked a little pale, and fidgeted nervously with the wires. Even the hardened Marshal was ill at ease, for a mere hanging was one thing, and this blasting of flesh and blood a very different one. As to the pressmen, their faces were whiter than the sheets which lay before them. The only man who appeared to feel none of the influence of these preparations was the little German crank, who strolled from one to the other with a smile on his lips and mischief in his eyes. More than once he even went so far as to burst into a shout of laughter, until the chaplain sternly rebuked him for his ill-timed levity.

"How can you so far forget yourself, Mr. Stulpnagel," said he, "as to jest in the presence of death?"

But the German was quite unabashed.

"If I were in the presence of death I should not jest," said he, "but since I am not I may do what I choose."

This flippant reply was about to draw another and a sterner reproof from the chaplain, when the door was swung open and two warders entered leading Duncan Warner between them. He glanced round him with a set face, stepped resolutely forward, and seated himself upon the chair.

"Touch her off!" said he.

It was barbarous to keep him in suspense. The chaplain murmured a few words in his ear, the attendant placed the cap upon his head, and then, while we all held our breath, the wire and the metal were brought in contact.

"Great Scott!" shouted Duncan Warner.

He had bounded in his chair as the frightful shock crashed through his system. But he was not dead. On the contrary, his eyes gleamed far more brightly than they had done before. There was only one change, but it was a singular one. The black had passed from his hair and beard as the shadow passes from a landscape. They were both as white as snow. And yet there was no other sign of decay. His skin was smooth and plump and lustrous as a child's.

The Marshal looked at the committee with a reproachful eye.

"There seems to be some hitch here, gentlemen," said he.

We three practical men looked at each other.

Peter Stulpnagel smiled pensively.

"I think that another one should do it," said I.

Again the connection was made, and again Duncan Warner sprang in his chair and shouted, but, indeed, were it not that he still remained in the chair none of us would have recognised him. His hair and his beard had shredded off in an instant, and the room looked like a barber's shop on a Saturday night. There he sat, his eyes still shining, his skin radiant with the glow of perfect health, but with a scalp as bald as a Dutch cheese, and a chin without so much as a trace of down. He began to revolve one of his arms, slowly and doubtfully at first, but with more confidence as he went on.

"That jint," said he, "has puzzled half the doctors on the Pacific Slope. It's as good as new, and as limber as a hickory twig."

"You are feeling pretty well?" asked the old German.

"Never better in my life," said Duncan Warner cheerily.

The situation was a painful one. The Marshal glared at the committee. Peter Stulpnagel grinned and rubbed his hands. The engineers scratched their heads. The bald-headed prisoner revolved his arm and looked pleased.

"I think that one more shock——" began the chairman.

"No, sir," said the Marshal "we've had foolery enough for one morning. We are here for an execution, and a execution we'll have."

"What do you propose?"

"There's a hook handy upon the ceiling. Fetch in a rope, and we'll soon set this matter straight."

There was another awkward delay while the warders departed for the cord. Peter Stulpnagel bent over Duncan Warner, and whispered something in his ear. The desperado started in surprise.

"You don't say?" he asked.

The German nodded.

"What! Noways?"

Peter shook his head, and the two began to laugh as though they shared some huge joke between them.

The rope was brought, and the Marshal himself slipped the noose over the criminal's neck. Then the two warders, the assistant and he swung their victim into the air. For half an hour he hung—a dreadful sight—from the ceiling.

Then in solemn silence they lowered him down, and one of the warders went out to order the shell to be brought round. But as he touched ground again what was our amazement when Duncan Warner put his hands up to his neck, loosened the noose, and took a long, deep breath.

"Paul Jefferson's sale is goin' well," he remarked, "I could see the crowd from up yonder," and he nodded at the hook in the ceiling.

"Up with him again!" shouted the Marshal, "we'll get the life out of him somehow."

In an instant the victim was up at the hook once more.

They kept him there for an hour, but when he came down he was perfectly garrulous.

"Old man Plunket goes too much to the Arcady Saloon," said he. "Three times he's been there in an hour; and him with a family. Old man Plunket would do well to swear off."

It was monstrous and incredible, but there it was. There was no getting round it. The man was there talking when he ought to have been dead. We all sat staring in amazement, but United States Marshal Carpenter was not a man to be euchred so easily. He motioned the others to one side, so that the prisoner was left standing alone.

"Duncan Warner," said he, slowly, "you are here to play your part, and I am here to play mine. Your game is to live if you can, and my game is to carry out the sentence of the law. You've beat us on electricity. I'll give you one there. And you've beat us on hanging, for you seem to thrive on it. But it's my turn to beat you now, for my duty has to be done."

He pulled a six-shooter from his coat as he spoke, and fired all the shots through the body of the prisoner. The room was so filled with smoke that we could see nothing, but when it cleared the prisoner was still standing there, looking down in disgust at the front of his coat.

"Coats must be cheap where you come from," said he. "Thirty dollars it cost me, and look at it now. The six holes in front are bad enough, but four of the balls have passed out, and a pretty state the back must be in."

The Marshal's revolver fell from his hand, and he dropped his arms to his sides, a beaten man.

"Maybe some of you gentlemen can tell me what this means," said he, looking helplessly at the committee.

Peter Stulpnagel took a step forward.

"I'll tell you all about it," said he.

"You seem to be the only person who knows anything."

"I AM the only person who knows anything. I should have warned these gentlemen; but, as they would not listen to me, I have allowed them to learn by experience. What you have done with your electricity is that you have increased this man's vitality until he can defy death for centuries."

"Centuries!"

"Yes, it will take the wear of hundreds of years to exhaust the enormous nervous energy with which you have drenched him. Electricity is life, and you have charged him with it to the utmost. Perhaps in fifty years you might execute him, but I am not sanguine about it."

"Great Scott! What shall I do with him?" cried the unhappy Marshal.

Peter Stulpnagel shrugged his shoulders.

"It seems to me that it does not much matter what you do with him now," said he.

"Maybe we could drain the electricity out of him again. Suppose we hang him up by the heels?"

"No, no, it's out of the question."

"Well, well, he shall do no more mischief in Los Amigos, anyhow," said the Marshal, with decision. "He shall go into the new gaol. The prison will wear him out."

"On the contrary," said Peter Stulpnagel, "I think that it is much more probable that he will wear out the prison."

It was rather a fiasco and for years we didn't talk more about it than we could help, but it's no secret now and I thought you might like to jot down the facts in your case-book.

THE DOCTORS OF HOYLAND.

Dr. James Ripley was always looked upon as an exceedingly lucky dog by all of the profession who knew him. His father had preceded him in a practice in the village of Hoyland, in the north of Hampshire, and all was ready for him on the very first day that the law allowed him to put his name at the foot of a prescription. In a few years the old gentleman retired, and settled on the South

Coast, leaving his son in undisputed possession of the whole country side. Save for Dr. Horton, near Basingstoke, the young surgeon had a clear run of six miles in every direction, and took his fifteen hundred pounds a year, though, as is usual in country practices, the stable swallowed up most of what the consulting-room earned.

Dr. James Ripley was two-and-thirty years of age, reserved, learned, unmarried, with set, rather stern features, and a thinning of the dark hair upon the top of his head, which was worth quite a hundred a year to him. He was particularly happy in his management of ladies. He had caught the tone of bland sternness and decisive suavity which dominates without offending. Ladies, however, were not equally happy in their management of him. Professionally, he was always at their service. Socially, he was a drop of quicksilver. In vain the country mammas spread out their simple lures in front of him. Dances and picnics were not to his taste, and he preferred during his scanty leisure to shut himself up in his study, and to bury himself in Virchow's Archives and the professional journals.

Study was a passion with him, and he would have none of the rust which often gathers round a country practitioner. It was his ambition to keep his knowledge as fresh and bright as at the moment when he had stepped out of the examination hall. He prided himself on being able at a moment's notice to rattle off the seven ramifications of some obscure artery, or to give the exact percentage of any physiological compound. After a long day's work he would sit up half the night performing iridectomies and extractions upon the sheep's eyes sent in by the village butcher, to the horror of his housekeeper, who had to remove the debris next morning. His love for his work was the one fanaticism which found a place in his dry, precise nature.

It was the more to his credit that he should keep up to date in his knowledge, since he had no competition to force him to exertion. In the seven years during which he had practised in Hoyland three rivals had pitted themselves against him, two in the village itself and one in the neighbouring hamlet of Lower Hoyland. Of these one had sickened and wasted, being, as it was said, himself the only patient whom he had treated during his eighteen months of ruralising. A second had bought a fourth share of a Basingstoke practice, and had departed honourably, while a third had vanished one September night, leaving a gutted house and an unpaid drug bill behind him. Since then the district had become a monopoly, and no one had dared to measure himself against the established fame of the Hoyland doctor.

It was, then, with a feeling of some surprise and considerable curiosity that on driving through Lower Hoyland one morning he perceived that the new house at the end of the village was occupied, and that a virgin brass plate glistened upon the swinging gate which faced the high road. He pulled up his fifty guinea chestnut mare and took a good look at it. "Verrinder Smith, M. D.," was printed across it in very neat, small lettering. The last man had had letters half a foot long, with a lamp like a fire-station. Dr. James Ripley noted the difference, and deduced from it that the new-comer might possibly prove a more formidable opponent. He was convinced of it that evening when he came to consult the current medical directory. By it he learned that Dr. Verrinder Smith was the holder of superb degrees, that he had studied with distinction at Edinburgh, Paris, Berlin, and Vienna, and finally that he had been awarded a gold medal and the Lee Hopkins scholarship for original research, in recognition of an exhaustive inquiry into the functions of the anterior spinal nerve roots. Dr. Ripley passed his fingers through his thin hair in bewilderment as he read his rival's record. What on earth could so brilliant a man mean by putting up his plate in a little Hampshire hamlet.

But Dr. Ripley furnished himself with an explanation to the riddle. No doubt Dr. Verrinder Smith had simply come down there in order to pursue some scientific research in peace and quiet. The plate was up as an address rather than as an invitation to patients. Of course, that must be the true explanation. In that case the presence of this brilliant neighbour would be a splendid thing for his own studies. He had often longed for some kindred mind, some steel on which he might strike his flint. Chance had brought it to him, and he rejoiced exceedingly.

And this joy it was which led him to take a step which was quite at variance with his usual habits. It is the custom for a new-comer among medical men to call first upon the older, and the etiquette upon the subject is strict. Dr. Ripley was pedantically exact on such points, and yet he deliberately drove over next day and called upon Dr. Verrinder Smith. Such a waiving of ceremony was, he felt, a gracious act upon his part, and a fit prelude to the intimate relations which he hoped to establish with his neighbour.

The house was neat and well appointed, and Dr. Ripley was shown by a smart maid into a dapper little consulting room. As he passed in he noticed two or three parasols and a lady's sun bonnet hanging in the hall. It was a pity that his colleague should be a married man. It would put them upon a different footing, and interfere with those long evenings of high scientific talk which he had pictured to himself. On the other hand, there was much in the consulting room to please him. Elaborate instruments, seen more often in hospitals than in the houses of private practitioners, were scattered about. A sphygmograph stood upon the table and a gasometer-like engine, which was new to Dr. Ripley, in the corner. A book-case full of ponderous volumes in French and German, paper-covered for the most part, and varying in tint from the shell to the yoke of a duck's egg, caught his wandering eyes, and he was deeply absorbed in their titles when the door opened suddenly behind him. Turning round, he found himself facing a little woman, whose plain, palish face was remarkable only for a pair of shrewd, humorous eyes of a blue which had two shades too much green in it. She held a pince-nez in her left hand, and the doctor's card in her right.

"How do you do, Dr. Ripley?" said she.

"How do you do, madam?" returned the visitor. "Your husband is perhaps out?"

"I am not married," said she simply.

"Oh, I beg your pardon! I meant the doctor—Dr. Verrinder Smith."

"I am Dr. Verrinder Smith."

Dr. Ripley was so surprised that he dropped his hat and forgot to pick it up again.

"What!" he grasped, "the Lee Hopkins prizeman! You!"

He had never seen a woman doctor before, and his whole conservative soul rose up in revolt at the idea. He could not recall any Biblical injunction that the man should remain ever the doctor and the woman the nurse, and yet he felt as if a blasphemy had been committed. His face betrayed his feelings only too clearly.

"I am sorry to disappoint you," said the lady drily.

"You certainly have surprised me," he answered, picking up his hat.

"You are not among our champions, then?"

"I cannot say that the movement has my approval."

"And why?"

"I should much prefer not to discuss it."

"But I am sure you will answer a lady's question."

"Ladies are in danger of losing their privileges when they usurp the place of the other sex. They cannot claim both."

"Why should a woman not earn her bread by her brains?"

Dr. Ripley felt irritated by the quiet manner in which the lady cross-questioned him.

"I should much prefer not to be led into a discussion, Miss Smith."

"Dr. Smith," she interrupted.

"Well, Dr. Smith! But if you insist upon an answer, I must say that I do not think medicine a suitable profession for women and that I have a personal objection to masculine ladies."

It was an exceedingly rude speech, and he was ashamed of it the instant after he had made it. The lady, however, simply raised her eyebrows and smiled.

"It seems to me that you are begging the question," said she. "Of course, if it makes women masculine that WOULD be a considerable deterioration."

It was a neat little counter, and Dr. Ripley, like a pinked fencer, bowed his acknowledgment.

"I must go," said he.

"I am sorry that we cannot come to some more friendly conclusion since we are to be neighbours," she remarked.

He bowed again, and took a step towards the door.

"It was a singular coincidence," she continued, "that at the instant that you called I was reading your paper on 'Locomotor Ataxia,' in the Lancet."

"Indeed," said he drily.

"I thought it was a very able monograph."

"You are very good."

"But the views which you attribute to Professor Pitres, of Bordeaux, have been repudiated by him."

"I have his pamphlet of 1890," said Dr. Ripley angrily.

"Here is his pamphlet of 1891." She picked it from among a litter of periodicals. "If you have time to glance your eye down this passage——"

Dr. Ripley took it from her and shot rapidly through the paragraph which she indicated. There was no denying that it completely knocked the bottom out of his own article. He threw it down, and with another frigid bow he made for the door. As he took the reins from the groom he glanced round and saw that the lady was standing at her window, and it seemed to him that she was laughing heartily.

All day the memory of this interview haunted him. He felt that he had come very badly out of it. She had showed herself to be his superior on his own pet subject. She had been courteous while he had been rude, self-possessed when he had been angry. And then, above all, there was her presence, her monstrous intrusion to rankle in his mind. A woman doctor had been an abstract thing before, repugnant but distant. Now she was there in actual practice, with a brass plate up just like his own, competing for the same patients. Not that he feared competition, but he objected to this lowering of his ideal of womanhood. She could not be more than thirty, and had a bright, mobile face, too. He thought of her humorous eyes, and of her strong, well-turned chin. It revolted him the more to recall the details of her education. A man, of course, could come through such an ordeal with all his purity, but it was nothing short of shameless in a woman.

But it was not long before he learned that even her competition was a thing to be feared. The novelty of her presence had brought a few curious invalids into her consulting rooms, and, once there, they had been so impressed by the firmness of her manner and by the singular, new-fashioned instruments with which she tapped, and peered, and sounded, that it formed the core of their conversation for weeks afterwards. And soon there were tangible proofs of her powers upon the country side. Farmer Eyton, whose callous ulcer had been quietly spreading over his shin for years back under a gentle regime of zinc ointment, was painted round with blistering fluid, and found, after three blasphemous nights, that his sore was stimulated into healing. Mrs. Crowder, who had always regarded the birthmark upon her second daughter Eliza as a sign of the indignation of the Creator at a third helping of raspberry tart which she had partaken of during a critical period, learned that, with the help of two galvanic needles, the mischief was not irreparable. In a month Dr. Verrinder Smith was known, and in two she was famous.

Occasionally, Dr. Ripley met her as he drove upon his rounds. She had started a high dogcart, taking the reins herself, with a little tiger behind. When they met he invariably raised his hat with punctilious politeness, but the grim severity of his face showed how formal was the courtesy. In fact, his dislike was rapidly deepening into absolute detestation. "The unsexed woman," was the description of her which he permitted himself to give to those of his patients who still remained staunch. But, indeed, they were a rapidly-decreasing body, and every day his pride was galled by the news of some fresh defection. The lady had somehow impressed the country folk with almost superstitious belief in her power, and from far and near they flocked to her consulting room.

But what galled him most of all was, when she did something which he had pronounced to be impracticable. For all his knowledge he lacked nerve as an operator, and usually sent his worst cases up to London. The lady, however, had no weakness of the sort, and took everything that came in her way. It was agony to him to hear that she was about to straighten little Alec Turner's club foot, and right at the fringe of the rumour came a note from his mother, the rector's wife, asking him if he would be so good as to act as chloroformist. It would be inhumanity to refuse, as there was no other who could take the place, but it was gall and wormwood to his sensitive nature. Yet, in spite of his vexation, he could not but admire the dexterity with which the thing was done. She handled the little wax-like foot so gently, and held the tiny tenotomy knife as an artist holds his pencil. One straight insertion, one snick of a tendon, and it was all over without a stain upon the white towel which lay beneath. He had never seen anything more masterly, and he had the honesty to say so, though her skill increased his dislike of her. The operation spread her fame still further at his expense, and self-preservation was added to his other grounds for detesting her. And this very detestation it was which brought matters to a curious climax.

One winter's night, just as he was rising from his lonely dinner, a groom came riding down from Squire Faircastle's, the richest man in the district, to say that his daughter had scalded her hand, and that medical help was needed on the instant. The coachman had ridden for the lady doctor, for it mattered nothing to the Squire who came as long as it were speedily. Dr. Ripley rushed from his surgery with the determination that she should not effect an entrance into this stronghold of his if hard driving on his part could prevent it. He did not even wait to light his lamps, but sprang into his gig and flew off as fast as hoof could rattle. He lived rather nearer to the Squire's than she did, and was convinced that he could get there well before her.

And so he would but for that whimsical element of chance, which will for ever muddle up the affairs of this world and dumbfound the prophets. Whether it came from the want of his lights, or from his mind being full of the thoughts of his rival, he allowed too little by half a foot in taking the sharp turn upon the Basingstoke road. The empty trap and the frightened horse clattered away into the darkness, while the Squire's groom crawled out of the ditch into which he had been shot. He struck a match, looked down at his groaning companion, and then, after the fashion of rough, strong men when they see what they have not seen before, he was very sick.

The doctor raised himself a little on his elbow in the glint of the match. He caught a glimpse of something white and sharp bristling through his trouser leg half way down the shin.

"Compound!" he groaned. "A three months' job," and fainted.

When he came to himself the groom was gone, for he had scudded off to the Squire's house for help, but a small page was holding a gig-lamp in front of his injured leg, and a woman, with an open case of polished instruments gleaming in the yellow light, was deftly slitting up his trouser with a crooked pair of scissors.

"It's all right, doctor," said she soothingly. "I am so sorry about it. You can have Dr. Horton to-morrow, but I am sure you will allow me to help you to-night. I could hardly believe my eyes when I saw you by the roadside."

"The groom has gone for help," groaned the sufferer.

"When it comes we can move you into the gig. A little more light, John! So! Ah, dear, dear, we shall have laceration unless we reduce this before we move you. Allow me to give you a whiff of chloroform, and I have no doubt that I can secure it sufficiently to——"

Dr. Ripley never heard the end of that sentence. He tried to raise a hand and to murmur something in protest, but a sweet smell was in his nostrils, and a sense of rich peace and lethargy stole over his jangled nerves. Down he sank, through clear, cool water, ever down and down into the green shadows beneath, gently, without effort, while the pleasant chiming of a great belfry rose and fell in his ears. Then he rose again, up and up, and ever up, with a terrible tightness about his temples, until at last he shot out of those green shadows and was in the light once more. Two bright, shining, golden spots gleamed before his dazed eyes. He blinked and blinked before he could give a name to them. They were only the two brass balls at the end posts of his bed, and he was lying in his own little room, with a head like a cannon ball, and a leg like an iron bar. Turning his eyes, he saw the calm face of Dr. Verrinder Smith looking down at him.

"Ah, at last!" said she. "I kept you under all the way home, for I knew how painful the jolting would be. It is in good position now with a strong side splint. I have ordered a morphia draught for you. Shall I tell your groom to ride for Dr. Horton in the morning?"

"I should prefer that you should continue the case," said Dr. Ripley feebly, and then, with a half hysterical laugh,—"You have all the rest of the parish as patients, you know, so you may as well make the thing complete by having me also."

It was not a very gracious speech, but it was a look of pity and not of anger which shone in her eyes as she turned away from his bedside.

Dr. Ripley had a brother, William, who was assistant surgeon at a London hospital, and who was down in Hampshire within a few hours of his hearing of the accident. He raised his brows when he heard the details.

"What! You are pestered with one of those!" he cried.

"I don't know what I should have done without her."

"I've no doubt she's an excellent nurse."

"She knows her work as well as you or I."

"Speak for yourself, James," said the London man with a sniff. "But apart from that, you know that the principle of the thing is all wrong."

"You think there is nothing to be said on the other side?"

"Good heavens! do you?"

"Well, I don't know. It struck me during the night that we may have been a little narrow in our views."

"Nonsense, James. It's all very fine for women to win prizes in the lecture room, but you know as well as I do that they are no use in an emergency. Now I warrant that this woman was all nerves when she was setting your leg. That reminds me that I had better just take a look at it and see that it is all right."

"I would rather that you did not undo it," said the patient. "I have her assurance that it is all right."

Brother William was deeply shocked.

"Of course, if a woman's assurance is of more value than the opinion of the assistant surgeon of a London hospital, there is nothing more to be said," he remarked.

"I should prefer that you did not touch it," said the patient firmly, and Dr. William went back to London that evening in a huff.

The lady, who had heard of his coming, was much surprised on learning his departure.

"We had a difference upon a point of professional etiquette," said Dr. James, and it was all the explanation he would vouchsafe.

For two long months Dr. Ripley was brought in contact with his rival every day, and he learned many things which he had not known before. She was a charming companion, as well as a most assiduous doctor. Her short presence during the long, weary day was like a flower in a sand waste. What interested him was precisely what interested her, and she could meet him at every point upon equal terms. And yet under all her learning and her firmness ran a sweet, womanly nature, peeping out in her talk, shining in her greenish eyes, showing itself in a thousand subtle ways which the dullest of men could read. And he, though a bit of a prig and a pedant, was by no means dull, and had honesty enough to confess when he was in the wrong.

"I don't know how to apologise to you," he said in his shame-faced fashion one day, when he had progressed so far as to be able to sit in an arm-chair with his leg upon another one; "I feel that I have been quite in the wrong."

"Why, then?"

"Over this woman question. I used to think that a woman must inevitably lose something of her charm if she took up such studies."

"Oh, you don't think they are necessarily unsexed, then?" she cried, with a mischievous smile.

"Please don't recall my idiotic expression."

"I feel so pleased that I should have helped in changing your views. I think that it is the most sincere compliment that I have ever had paid me."

"At any rate, it is the truth," said he, and was happy all night at the remembrance of the flush of pleasure which made her pale face look quite comely for the instant.

For, indeed, he was already far past the stage when he would acknowledge her as the equal of any other woman. Already he could not disguise from himself that she had become the one woman. Her dainty skill, her gentle touch, her sweet presence, the community of their tastes, had all united to hopelessly upset his previous opinions. It was a dark day for him now when his convalescence allowed her to miss a visit, and darker still that other one which he saw approaching when all occasion for her visits would be at an end. It came round at last, however, and he felt that his whole life's fortune would hang upon the issue of that final interview. He was a direct man by nature, so he laid his hand upon hers as it felt for his pulse, and he asked her if she would be his wife.

"What, and unite the practices?" said she.

He started in pain and anger.

"Surely you do not attribute any such base motive to me!" he cried. "I love you as unselfishly as ever a woman was loved."

"No, I was wrong. It was a foolish speech," said she, moving her chair a little back, and tapping her stethoscope upon her knee. "Forget that I ever said it. I am so sorry to cause you any disappointment, and I appreciate most highly the honour which you do me, but what you ask is quite impossible."

With another woman he might have urged the point, but his instincts told him that it was quite useless with this one. Her tone of voice was conclusive. He said nothing, but leaned back in his chair a stricken man.

"I am so sorry," she said again. "If I had known what was passing in your mind I should have told you earlier that I intended to devote my life entirely to science. There are many women with a capacity for marriage, but few with a taste for biology. I will remain true to my own line, then. I came down here while waiting for an opening in the Paris Physiological Laboratory. I have just heard that there is a vacancy for me there, and so you will be troubled no more by my intrusion upon your practice. I have done you an injustice just as you did me one. I thought you narrow and pedantic, with no good quality. I have learned during your illness to appreciate you better, and the recollection of our friendship will always be a very pleasant one to me."

And so it came about that in a very few weeks there was only one doctor in Hoyland. But folks noticed that the one had aged many years in a few months, that a weary sadness lurked always in the depths of his blue eyes, and that he was less concerned than ever with the eligible young ladies whom chance, or their careful country mammas, placed in his way.

THE SURGEON TALKS.

"Men die of the diseases which they have studied most," remarked the surgeon, snipping off the end of a cigar with all his professional neatness and finish. "It's as if the morbid condition was an evil creature which, when it found itself closely hunted, flew at the throat of its pursuer. If you worry the microbes too much they may worry you. I've seen cases of it, and not necessarily in microbic diseases either. There was, of course, the well-known instance of Liston and the aneurism; and a dozen others that I could mention. You couldn't have a clearer case than that of poor old Walker of St. Christopher's. Not heard of it? Well, of course, it was a little before your time, but I wonder that it should have been forgotten. You youngsters are so busy in keeping up to the day that you lose a good deal that is interesting of yesterday.

"Walker was one of the best men in Europe on nervous disease. You must have read his little book on sclerosis of the posterior columns. It's as interesting as a novel, and epoch-making in its way. He worked like a horse, did Walker—huge consulting practice—hours a day in the clinical wards—constant original investigations. And then he enjoyed himself also. 'De mortuis,' of course, but still it's an open secret among all who knew him. If he died at forty-five, he crammed eighty years into it. The marvel was that he could have held on so long at the pace at which he was going. But he took it beautifully when it came.

"I was his clinical assistant at the time. Walker was lecturing on locomotor ataxia to a wardful of youngsters. He was explaining that one of the early signs of the complaint was that the patient could not put his heels together with his eyes shut without staggering. As he spoke, he suited the action to the word. I don't suppose the boys noticed anything. I did, and so did he, though he finished his lecture without a sign.

"When it was over he came into my room and lit a cigarette.

"'Just run over my reflexes, Smith,' said he.

"There was hardly a trace of them left. I tapped away at his knee-tendon and might as well have tried to get a jerk out of that sofa-cushion. He stood with his eyes shut again, and he swayed like a bush in the wind.

"'So,' said he, 'it was not intercostal neuralgia after all.'

"Then I knew that he had had the lightning pains, and that the case was complete. There was nothing to say, so I sat looking at him while he puffed and puffed at his cigarette. Here he was, a man in the prime of life, one of the handsomest men in London, with money, fame, social success, everything at his feet, and now, without a moment's warning, he was told that inevitable death lay before him, a death accompanied by more refined and lingering tortures than if he were bound upon a Red Indian stake. He sat in the middle of the blue cigarette cloud with his eyes cast down, and the slightest little tightening of his lips. Then he rose with a motion of his arms, as one who throws off old thoughts and enters upon a new course.

"'Better put this thing straight at once,' said he. 'I must make some fresh arrangements. May I use your paper and envelopes?'

"He settled himself at my desk and he wrote half a dozen letters. It is not a breach of confidence to say that they were not addressed to his professional brothers. Walker was a single man, which means that he was not restricted to a single woman. When he had finished, he walked out of that little room of mine, leaving every hope and ambition of his life behind him. And he might have had another year of ignorance and peace if it had not been for the chance illustration in his lecture.

"It took five years to kill him, and he stood it well. If he had ever been a little irregular he atoned for it in that long martyrdom. He kept an admirable record of his own symptoms, and worked out the eye changes more fully than has ever been done. When the ptosis got very bad he would hold his eyelid up with one hand while he wrote. Then, when he could not co-ordinate his muscles to write, he dictated to his nurse. So died, in the odour of science, James Walker, aet. 45.

"Poor old Walker was very fond of experimental surgery, and he broke ground in several directions. Between ourselves, there may have been some more ground-breaking afterwards, but he did his best for his cases. You know

M'Namara, don't you? He always wears his hair long. He lets it be understood that it comes from his artistic strain, but it is really to conceal the loss of one of his ears. Walker cut the other one off, but you must not tell Mac I said so.

"It was like this. Walker had a fad about the portio dura—the motor to the face, you know—and he thought paralysis of it came from a disturbance of the blood supply. Something else which counterbalanced that disturbance might, he thought, set it right again. We had a very obstinate case of Bell's paralysis in the wards, and had tried it with every conceivable thing, blistering, tonics, nerve-stretching, galvanism, needles, but all without result. Walker got it into his head that removal of the ear would increase the blood supply to the part, and he very soon gained the consent of the patient to the operation.

"Well, we did it at night. Walker, of course, felt that it was something of an experiment, and did not wish too much talk about it unless it proved successful. There were half-a-dozen of us there, M'Namara and I among the rest. The room was a small one, and in the centre was in the narrow table, with a macintosh over the pillow, and a blanket which extended almost to the floor on either side. Two candles, on a side-table near the pillow, supplied all the light. In came the patient, with one side of his face as smooth as a baby's, and the other all in a quiver with fright. He lay down, and the chloroform towel was placed over his face, while Walker threaded his needles in the candle light. The chloroformist stood at the head of the table, and M'Namara was stationed at the side to control the patient. The rest of us stood by to assist.

"Well, the man was about half over when he fell into one of those convulsive flurries which come with the semi-unconscious stage. He kicked and plunged and struck out with both hands. Over with a crash went the little table which held the candles, and in an instant we were left in total darkness. You can think what a rush and a scurry there was, one to pick up the table, one to find the matches, and some to restrain the patient who was still dashing himself about. He was held down by two dressers, the chloroform was pushed, and by the time the candles were relit, his incoherent, half-smothered shoutings had changed to a stertorous snore. His head was turned on the pillow and the towel was still kept over his face while the operation was carried through. Then the towel was withdrawn, and you can conceive our amazement when we looked upon the face of M'Namara.

"How did it happen? Why, simply enough. As the candles went over, the chloroformist had stopped for an instant and had tried to catch them. The patient, just as the light went out, had rolled off and under the table. Poor M'Namara, clinging frantically to him, had been dragged across it, and the chloroformist, feeling him there, had naturally claped the towel across his mouth and nose. The others had secured him, and the more he roared and kicked the more they drenched him with chloroform. Walker was very nice about it, and made the most handsome apologies. He offered to do a plastic on the spot, and make as good an ear as he could, but M'Namara had had enough of it. As to the patient, we found him sleeping placidly under the table, with the ends of the blanket screening him on both sides. Walker sent M'Namara round his ear next day in a jar of methylated spirit, but Mac's wife was very angry about it, and it led to a good deal of ill-feeling.

"Some people say that the more one has to do with human nature, and the closer one is brought in contact with it, the less one thinks of it. I don't believe that those who know most would uphold that view. My own experience is dead against it. I was brought up in the miserable-mortal-clay school of theology, and yet here I am, after thirty years of intimate acquaintance with humanity, filled with respect for it. The evil lies commonly upon the surface. The deeper strata are good. A hundred times I have seen folk condemned to death as suddenly as poor Walker was. Sometimes it was to blindness or to mutilations which are worse than death. Men and women, they almost all took it beautifully, and some with such lovely unselfishness, and with such complete absorption in the thought of how their fate would affect others, that the man about town, or the frivolously-dressed woman has seemed to change into an angel before my eyes. I have seen death-beds, too, of all ages and of all creeds and want of creeds. I never saw any of them shrink, save only one poor, imaginative young fellow, who had spent his blameless life in the strictest of sects. Of course, an exhausted frame is incapable of fear, as anyone can vouch who is told, in the midst of his sea-sickness, that the ship is going to the bottom. That is why I rate courage in the face of mutilation to be higher than courage when a wasting illness is fining away into death.

"Now, I'll take a case which I had in my own practice last Wednesday. A lady came in to consult me—the wife of a well-known sporting baronet. The husband had come with her, but remained, at her request, in the waiting-room. I need not go into details, but it proved to be a peculiarly malignant case of cancer. 'I knew it,' said she. 'How long have I to live?' 'I fear that it may exhaust your strength in a few months,' I answered. 'Poor old Jack!' said she. 'I'll tell him that it is not dangerous.' 'Why should you deceive him?' I asked. 'Well, he's very uneasy about it, and he is quaking now in the waiting-room. He has two old friends to dinner to-night, and I haven't the heart to spoil his evening. To-morrow will be time enough for him to learn the truth.' Out she walked, the brave little woman, and a moment later her husband, with his big, red face shining with joy came plunging into my room to shake me by the hand. No, I respected her wish and I did not undeceive him. I dare bet that evening was one of the brightest, and the next morning the darkest, of his life.

"It's wonderful how bravely and cheerily a woman can face a crushing blow. It is different with men. A man can stand it without complaining, but it knocks him dazed and silly all the same. But the woman does not lose her wits any more than she does her courage. Now, I had a case only a few weeks ago which would show you what I mean. A gentleman consulted me about his wife, a very beautiful woman. She had a small tubercular nodule upon her upper arm, according to him. He was sure that it was of no importance, but he wanted to know whether Devonshire or the Riviera would be the better for her. I examined her and found a frightful sarcoma of the bone, hardly showing upon the surface, but involving the shoulder-blade and clavicle as well as the humerus. A more malignant case I have never seen. I sent her out of the room and I told him the truth. What did he do? Why, he walked slowly round that room with his hands behind his back, looking with the greatest interest at the pictures. I can see him now, putting up his gold pince-nez and staring at them with perfectly vacant eyes, which told me that he saw neither them nor the wall behind them. 'Amputation of the arm?' he asked at last. 'And of the collar-bone and shoulder-blade,' said I. 'Quite so. The collar-bone and shoulder-blade,' he repeated, still staring about him with those lifeless eyes. It settled him. I don't believe he'll ever be the same man again. But the woman took it as bravely and brightly as could be, and she has done very well since. The mischief was so great that the arm snapped as we drew it from the night-dress. No, I don't think that there will be any return, and I have every hope of her recovery.

"The first patient is a thing which one remembers all one's life. Mine was commonplace, and the details are of no interest. I had a curious visitor, however, during the first few months after my plate went up. It was an elderly woman, richly dressed, with a wickerwork picnic basket in her hand. This she opened with the tears streaming down her face, and out there waddled the fattest, ugliest, and mangiest little pug dog that I have ever seen. 'I wish you to put him painlessly out of the world, doctor,' she cried. 'Quick, quick, or my resolution may give way.' She flung herself down, with hysterical sobs, upon the sofa. The less experienced a doctor is, the higher are his notions of professional dignity, as I need not remind you, my young friend, so I was about to refuse the commission with indignation, when I bethought me that, quite apart from medicine, we were gentleman and lady, and that she had asked me to do something for her which was evidently of the greatest possible importance in her eyes. I led off the poor little doggie, therefore, and with the help of a saucerful of milk and a few drops of prussic acid his exit was as speedy and painless as could be desired. 'Is it over?' she cried as I entered. It was really tragic to see how all the love which should have gone to husband and children had, in default of them, been centred upon this uncouth little animal. She left, quite broken down, in her carriage, and it was only after her departure that I saw an envelope sealed with a large red seal, and lying upon the blotting pad of my desk. Outside, in pencil, was written: 'I have no doubt that you would willingly have done this without a fee, but I insist upon your acceptance of the enclosed.' I opened it with some vague notions of an eccentric millionaire and a fifty-pound note, but all I found was a postal order for four and sixpence. The whole incident struck me as so whimsical that I laughed until I was tired. You'll find there's so much tragedy in a doctor's life, my boy, that he would not be able to stand it if it were not for the strain of comedy which comes every now and then to leaven it.

"And a doctor has very much to be thankful for also. Don't you ever forget it. It is such a pleasure to do a little good that a man should pay for the privilege instead of being paid for it. Still, of course, he has his home to keep up and his wife and children to support. But his patients are his friends—or they should be so. He goes from house to house, and his step and his voice are loved and welcomed in each. What could a man ask for more than that? And besides, he is forced to be a good man. It is impossible for him to be anything else. How can a man spend his whole life in seeing suffering bravely borne and yet remain a hard or a vicious man? It is a noble, generous, kindly profession, and you youngsters have got to see that it remains so."

www.ingramcontent.com/pod-product-compliance
Lightning Source LLC
LaVergne TN
LVHW040101080526
838202LV00045B/3723